AF417006

Praise for
An Olympian Hike: The Adventures of a Rookie Camper in the Woods

"If you have any thoughts about going camping and/or hiking, you need to read this book. The author is excellent in the role of the storyteller, and covers such topics as:

- *Preparation, or lack thereof;*
- *The necessary clothing, or lack thereof;*
- *The proper nutrition, or lack thereof;*
- *Cleanliness, or lack thereof;*
- *And many more aspects of a first camping/hiking adventure in the Olympic mountains of Washington.*

His style, in a dry, extremely humorous manner, will keep you highly entertained. And while I will admit to losing my sense of smell and taste (non-Covid related), I flatly deny my urine ever tested "two plus for pepperoni"!

~~ **Robert Todd**, long-time business associate, friend, and critic …

"Book #4, as he calls it, is reminiscent of sitting around a camp fire with friends telling stories of past adventures. His tales are plausible which keeps you wondering which scenarios really happened to him and which ones were tall tales."

~~ ***Leah Craig***, friend and acupuncturist …

"If I were that Bill guy, after reading this Tale, I'd be saying: 'WHAT THE HELL WAS I THINKING?! taking a Tenderfoot on a Trek like that?' It's EVidence of a benevolent universe that no one got permanently maimed on that adventure. As Rumi might have said, 'Chase a deer, end up everywhere.' Colt chases adventure and is allowed to wander a magnificent stretch of the Olympic outback, managing to escape with more stories than bruises. A skilled raconteur, Ev translates Colt's (mis)adventures into an inspiring tale that somehow ends not in woe, but in grace."

~~ ***Bill Fleming***, veteran hiker, camper and climber and a contributor to 'Olympic Mountains Trail Guide' by Robert L. Wood

"If Charles Dickens decided to go camping and then decided to write a story about it, that's what the author has done here, and it's really fun! Such a unique voice and a wonderful tale told from a narrator's voice that just works in unexpected ways from page one all the way to the end!"

~~ **D. D. Scott**, International Bestselling Author

An Olympian Hike:
The Adventures of a Rookie Camper in the Woods

A Novel

by

Everett Kunzelman

LETLOVEGLOW
AUTHOR SERVICES
BY D. D. SCOTT

Contents

PART II: THE BIG EVENT
(Hiking and Camping in the Olympic Mountains)

63

Chapter Nine:

Finally, Heading Toward the Wild

65

Chapter Ten:

To the Woods …

75

Chapter Eleven:

Going Up

87

Chapter Twelve:

Late July/Early August/Summer Snow Fall

99

Preface

>⊨——▶

You are about to read an unusual novel. It involves narration by a storyteller (that would be me) and characters living their parts, in action and conversation. Most novels do not have a "preface" or any introductory comments explaining the journey on which you are about to embark. This one, however, might benefit you, the reader, by including at least some introductory remarks. The excursion you're about to go on takes on more understanding with a little explanation. (Besides, my editor told me to write one.)

The book is about Colton, who hired me as his storyteller to help him share his likely embellished adventure from several years ago in the Olympic Mountains. The early chapters contain partial truths about his life which then lead to his Olympic adventure story, making the novel based on at least some historic reality as its foundation. Then, there is the big event – hiking and camping in the mountains. Finally, there is Colton's life afterwards, where he returns to some normalcy, using his odyssey to come to some life conclusions.

His adventure is better understood with some preliminary background information (or backstory, as it's referred to in writer's circles). As your storyteller, I need to lay the groundwork for how his exploit even came into being, which helps the entire story eventually unfold. So, this backstory is contained in the first several chapters that lead up to the actual hiking/camping event. Colton's pre-story attempts to make sense of his interest in even trying to establish and then complete a goal that he made. Some of the early chapters have an accurate history of the person we call Colton (or so he says), but there also seems to be exaggerations and fictional accounts tossed in for good measure. (Note: This storyteller now knows Colton somewhat better, and I can sense when the truth becomes coated with some dressing, if you will.)

Then … there is the actual camping and hiking tale itself, the basis for the book. Listening to Colton makes me think there is more fiction here than in the pre-story we managed to construct, but that said, there are a few actual historical details as well. Colton remembers what he can, and he enhances everything else.

The final chapters deal with his post-woods experience – like him getting home and then various happenings afterward that relate to his Olympic experience. Colton was almost "on a roll", rambling about his adventure, trying to make sense of the whole tale. Perhaps he was tying loose ends together in hopes of achieving a few meaningful conclusions.

Colton, with my help, weaves the tale you are about to read, connecting the various parts, as required, so that there really is an appearance of one story being told. If Colton himself had just spun the tale, there definitely would have been holes and splinters and tangents. Though, I admit, some of those make the book more interesting to me and thus have been retained from my interviews of him. After all, this guy Colton did experience something out there in the mountains and woods. There is some reality presented – or so he says.

Anyway, let's dive into the account and see where the presumed chronicle, as well as the actual yarn, take you, starting well before the woods' encounter in Colton's early days of life

…

PART I

COLTON'S EARLY DAYS

(i.e.: Colton's Backstory)

6

Chapter One

A Prologue –

Introductions, Goals, How Did We Get Here?

Setting goals comes easy for many people. Accomplishing them is usually more difficult ... for most.

To understand the possible truth in the statements above, consider any New Year's resolution as a goal. The "setting the goal" is in fact easy, but the "accomplishing" part? Not nearly as easy. Probably why the gyms are basically empty by mid-February, and the ice cream and candy stores begin a rebirth.

For Colton – "no last name, please", he insisted – I, the storyteller, explained that the name "Colton" was not common enough that people wouldn't know who he was when presented the details. The facts would come together. His identification would be complete. Everyone he knew would figure out that he was "that Colton" in this tale. Well, he still wanted to use "Colton", regardless of my reasoning. So, we will.

"Let's not nail down the identity with the last name," he said.

Okay … we can try. Perhaps "Colton" is his "stage name". Or "want-to-be-stage-name". Not his "real" name. Yeah, we'll go with the first option, for now.

Where were we?

For Colton, setting goals was more difficult than for many people. Or so he thought. The decision to have a goal seemed to be somewhat easier for him than actually going ahead and setting one, which created an obligation and thus the beginning of trouble for Colton. That said, he could always decide not to have the goal any longer, if the planning of achieving it got out of hand.

To create a goal seemed more likely for Colton if he had a list of possibilities, although that wasn't necessarily true, either. Having one in mind, though, might get the ball rolling, but then that would mean he had to first define and name the goal, which would certainly involve what the goal was to be, but also a myriad of other details that could include variations of when, how, where, why, and possibly who was involved, with all sorts of specific attributes. Defining a goal could get a little complicated for Colton, you see.

Beyond that, a goal may need to have some valuable characteristics. That would include achievability and, possibly, measurability. If Colton couldn't possibly achieve his objective, the goal itself was pointless, and he could set it aside right then and there, or as soon as the unachievable characteristic was apparent to him. Could be a while, I suppose. There could also be differences of opinion on the probability of success from his friends and family. The measurement of said goal could be relative to a deadline. Depends on the formality of the goal and how quantitative it was to begin with. Then there was the commitment to the goal. That included setting a plan in motion, getting any requirements in place, and moving any obstacles out of the way.

And you thought he could just decide "I'm going to do this or that"! Oh, he could. Might work. Most goals, however, probably have more complexity. Many, I suspect however, are not seen as quite so convoluted.

So, in this story, Colton set a goal ... kind of. And we will get back to that ... eventually.

Colton's life story is interesting, at least to him. Parts of it could be considered as such for others. Maybe some of it will be to you, the reader. (Hope so – he had to pay me to tell his story ...) His life could be described as a weaving or braiding of cooked noodles. In other words, there's not much holding the whole thing securely together. This is due to his rather loose approach to life and his similar approach to goals, in general. (There will be more in this story about noodles. Could be too much, but then again, maybe more could be said about those slippery tricksters too. And it could be symbolic, by definition, if I'm being highly literary about it.)

Part of Colton's story could also be that of a fallen pleb who rose to some sort of exceptionalism quite by accident – being in the right place at the right time with just the right skills and knowing just the right people. Actually … that is more or less generally true of his entire life. And the "fallen" aspect of Colton "the fallen pleb" will gain traction later where and when traction was lost. Stay tuned.

Colton thought there would be some fun in writing a book. He wanted to write about his dogs – Indy and Myna – and tell their stories. Or find a person who would be his "storyteller", who he could tell about "the girls" (the dogs), and the storyteller could just write down the entire tale. Colton would get the "as told by" credit.

As noted earlier, I'm the storyteller. He confided in me to deliver the product of this book. And I learned everything about his dogs … constantly … and I mean everything … not a bone unturned (pun intended). Although the dogs were a tremendous part of his life prior to retirement, the three of them became inseparable when work had pretty much passed Colton by.

But there really was a better story than that of Colton's "girls" …

The greater and more intriguing adventure was the tale of his trails in the Washington State woods versus his tales (and tails) in the city and the Indiana woods. Colton did, however, figure out a way to have his dogs mentioned by this storyteller (me) now and then, for which he can take credit … after all, many people like dogs. (Might have been a wonderful effort to tell dog stories and be rewarded by huge sales of his book, but, no – this is the "participation ribbon" account that will illustrate life as it is known to Colton.)

Note: He didn't want me to use the dogs' names – not sure why – just wanted them mentioned, but I felt like they had to have more of an identity. Mission accomplished on that – at least they have names, whether correct or not. And we're just getting started.

The chronicle of Colton's life could go back prior to his conception, with all sorts of anecdotal half-truths and guesses and misconceptions (not his – he was conceived, after all). But there may have been all sorts of happenings that are of importance to his life … I don't know. But I can tell you that there was a bevy of information pulled from partial reality.

Sometimes you hear what you want to hear. Or understand what you want to understand. Or remember what you want to remember. I, your storyteller, am certainly guilty of that. That said, we all are … well, a large percentage of us are, anyway.

Colton was no different. And that is why we have ourselves a story to be told that is not necessarily a historical account. And that is also the reason there is an assist coming for the boy in the form of a "real" hero we will call "Bill", who will be helping out our "fictional" character, Colton.

Colton thought that "Bill" was a fitting name for the champion of the story. Our hero knows the trails, the mountains, and the campsites. Bill knows most everything there is to know about the Olympic Mountains, the Olympic National Forest, and Olympic National Park, as well as the Cascades and possibly even the Green Mountains. All of which took Colton years to figure out even part of. Colton's either slow or he never asked the right questions. That, or he simply didn't take the time to comprehend the correct answers or acquire all the facts. Could be that he just presumed too much. Or … he didn't listen well. But this story isn't to excessively praise Bill, despite desiring to give him his just desserts, but rather it's to shine a light on Bill's rattled partner in the adventure, Colton, who finally set a goal in motion and made the commitment to attempt to achieve it.

So, we will tell a story about Colton, remembering that Bill is the reason Colton survived to then enlist the aid of this storyteller to share his role in a goal determined to be achieved by Colton. Having heard the story a few times, a few dozen or more, actually a whole lot more than that, this was really fun for me, the storyteller, to find the middle ground where reality seems to dwell, but not entirely. At least Colton allowed this storyteller to write the story as I saw the tale. Risky …

The success for Colton? No trophy, but rather a placemark. A participation ribbon for his awkward attempt. But there life goes … and Colton did survive the adventure we will get to telling now. So, that's a plus.

Once upon a time…

Chapter Two

The Height-Challenged Non-Athlete

Colton was short as a child. Colton was short as a teen. Colton was short as a young to middle-aged adult.

Colton was short. Still is. He looks up to a lot of people. Scratch that … most people – he looks up to most people. He and I see eye-to-eye. Literally. In other respects, besides our identical lines of sight, the jury is out.

Short. Let's make that "relatively short" and not for the image or mental disposition of the storyteller (I have no concern with the label). Being five-foot-six or thereabouts, not likely plus, more likely minus, isn't exactly the height considered to be a dwarf. Golly, there were a bunch of people shorter than Colton, even a couple, if he recalled correctly, in professional basketball.

Stories from the early days of his life, however, amplified the height issue for him. His grandma told him he walked at six months of age. Perhaps he did. But that really had nothing to do with his height. Well, except that she also said he was able to walk, fully upright, all the way under the kitchen table without hitting his head or ducking. No pictures. No movies. No proof. But that's what Grandma said, so it must be true. Not to say she was exaggerating. Could be one hundred percent true, and Grandma tended to be a teller of truth, the whole truth, and nothing but the truth – as she knew or understood what truth was, according to Colton.

Early pictures Colton recovered suggest there was a distinct possibility of his under-the-table walking capability. One picture, when just a little older than Grandma reported (a year to one-and-a-half years old possibly) shows him at no more than about 26 or so inches tall, give or take a few, hard to say for sure. He wasn't photographed at one of those restaurants or stores or gas stations with a height chart by the door. His height as illustrated in the picture noted was short enough to wander about the kitchen without bumping his head. I can add, if he allows this observation to stay in the story, that I had a similar outfit in a picture of me when I was a youngster. Just found that interesting.

In trying to understand how he could have a dad over six feet and still be so height-challenged perplexed Colton. Then, he remembered his mom was barely five-feet tall. Quite possibly, his mom's genetics had kicked in.

The significance of his height challenge is most fondly recalled from his high school gym class. Gentlemen and ladies had separate classes in those days. (That was a while back.) The guys (I mean "gentlemen") were all lined up from tallest to shortest. Colton can't recall why they did that. The seven-footer in his class obviously stood out. Anyway, Colton seemed to recall that he was third from the end. Yeah … on the short end. Or was that fourth from the end? Regardless, Colton doesn't think he was the shortest. He was still on his way to five-foot-six, though – not quite there yet. That took a while. A few years longer. Could be several years more.

In addition to his height issue, there was intimidation to deal with. Walking down the long hall to the gym and locker rooms took Colton past trophy cases of champions, both teams and individuals. Representatives of his high school had done well in various state championships over the years, but there he was, merely walking in the hallway, not part of its hallowed décor. Some of the trophies themselves might have been as tall as him.

Regardless of stories about his youth and height obstacles, there was little doubt of his dunking capability on the basketball court – or lack thereof. Or his shooting proficiency. He couldn't dribble either. Or pass. Or easily catch any passes. "Assists" would depend on your perspective and definition of the concept. "Turnovers" … oh, those he could do. And he grew up in a basketball crazy state … and went to a basketball crazy high school and continued on to a basketball crazy university. It was all nuts! How could not even a little aspect of basketball rub off on him?! But, it sure wasn't guaranteed, and we have our proof in Colton.

Nevertheless, every now and then Col (as he was known by some friends) would play basketball with other people. Not shooting by himself, but on an actual team. Never a formal team – always a pick-up game. Still, there were sides. A competition.

Teams. No uniforms. He could not tell me if they were "shirts and skins" games. Claimed he couldn't remember.

Back in school, in gym class, when the captains – that would be two of the jocks – picked their teams for basketball or any other competition, there was a long wait until Colton heard his name called. Let's just say that he had time to count the big lights in the gym, count the panes of glass in the windows and doors, the steps to the top of the bleachers. He didn't like to talk a lot about all that and never did admit to knowing the number of lights … or panes of glass … or steps. Sometimes, though, he excitedly recalled being selected for a team – as was everyone else in the class, eventually.

Col's last experience at basketball was a pick-up game with people at work in his late 40's. As he remembers the experience, a group met some place near the office at a sports center once a week to play. For some reason, he was invited, a surprise right there, and he played once, that he remembers. One time. And that was the time he had a pass go to him that was partially deflected, and the ball nailed the end of his right thumb. He had lived almost to age 50 with no broken bones … until that pass.

Oh, sure – you can argue that the pass wasn't deflected. But, it was. He is absolutely certain of that. Positive. No doubt in his mind. It was not that he misjudged the catch. Not at all.

Over twenty years later, his thumb still hurts.

Beyond basketball, he tells of living in his late twenties across the street from a guy who would get with friends at his place of work and their friends and play tackle football. Colton went once to join in. One time. Guess who was smallest? When

Col (or Colt to some) talks about that pick-up game, which is rare, he recalls everyone being way too serious. The atmosphere was as if that game were the Super Bowl. The game might have been *their* Super Bowl. Not that there was any money involved that he knew of. There was an early play, trying to figure out how to use the scrawny neighbor of a friend, when they had Col hike the ball. He missed the count, and they then assigned him to essentially play right field in a football game. Basically, he was to carry water, keep score, and stay out of the way.

Now all this said about the disadvantages of being on the short end, shorter people can sometimes move pretty fast. They have to. They have to avoid being crushed by those on the larger end. And Colton loved tackle football! He loved to "hit" people – or play defense – but he also loved to carry the ball. That's where his speed helped him as well. In either defense or offense, he could move pretty fast.

That ability apparently evaporated by age thirty. Or maybe it was at twenty-five. Either way, it was definitely gone by his Super Bowl appearance.

He claims to have run the hundred-yard dash as a teen in about 10.5 seconds. Or so. Was it 11.5 seconds? Or so. The exact timing escapes him. And that was never done in full football gear. In fact, he never was in full football gear. Never timed in a forty.

He told me he did go fast in a car once. He told me about driving an Indy car. That was about six months before his sixtieth birthday. So what, you might be asking? Well … that did not seem to be important to this story until Colton added a "little" detail in passing. As some of you may know, Indy car drivers are reportedly short. Some aren't, but some are. Anyway, he had the chance to drive an Indy car at the Indianapolis Motor Speedway, less than a couple of miles from where he said he grew up. It was never so much a goal of his as it was a dream – one he figured would never happen. Circumstances developed, though, which led to that exciting opportunity materializing. And there was even one fact of interest relating to his height that called for inclusion right here in his story: He was short enough that they had to use some sort of extra padding behind him in the seat so that his feet could touch the pedals (and push them down). Enough said about that, I suppose.

So yeah, Colton (Col/Colt) was small. Or short. Both, at times, may have been true. "Small" did not get him a lot of press … usually. No adult guardian would sign for him to play sports in high school. They didn't want him hurt. Or crushed. So, despite his speed – not the fastest, but faster than many in his class, or so he says (again) – the life of a non-athlete was his. He was a student. Not student athlete.

And that was perfectly fine. His life was good. Still is. Except for his thumb.

Chapter Three

Hiking Means Snakes in the Parks, Snakes in the Road, Snakes in the Yard

Colt, as you may recall from earlier, had been walking since he was six months of age. Given how old he is today, that's a lot of walking. I won't say for sure how old that is. You might be able to figure that out from a few of the fun facts later presented. Regardless, he has a high total step count in life.

Weekends as a kid were without the necessity of any strength training or whatever else student athletes did. So, he had all the time in the world. And while there was little money to do a lot, the kids who ran together always seemed to find at least a couple or so drivers in the mix to venture out to the state parks once in a while to walk the trails.

Hiking. That's what was going on. Hiking. It was beyond simple walking. It was Hiking. They're not the same, at all. And Colton loved this hiking thing. He seemed to be pretty adept at taking the smaller hills, upslopes and descents. His footing appeared to be decent and that kept him upright. No crawling, falling, whatever.

Lucky for him, his home state had (and still has) a lot of great state parks and other great places where a bunch of kids or adults or both could venture out into the woods for a stroll.

Even his walk to high school was potentially an exciting hike! He claims to have taken the dead end of his home street, crossed a somewhat busy street, and then turned left through a path (or trail) into some shrubs and trees, including a fair number of honey locust trees (meaning there were big thorns even directly out of the tree trunks). Only the adventurous would walk through that area which had the smell of rubber and oil as it was located behind several light industrial companies, like auto repair places, battery shops and such. Eventually, one would pop out next to the train yards.

So, yes. There was trespassing. And it was likely done through some hazardous wastes. (That said, Colt doesn't recall his shoes glowing in the dark).

Aside from the honey locust trees and the hazardous wastes, there's not much else Colt recalls about that "trail." He was never called out for being on that well-worn path by anyone working at the companies or the railroad. He never ran into hobos from the trains asking about "rooms to let for fifty cents" or anything like that. He did tell me about one guy who stopped by his house once asking if there was any work he could do for a few dollars. He offered to cut grass, pick up limbs, pick weeds, clean up outside, anything. Grandma told him no, but she did ask if he was hungry. He said he was, so she gave him a dark pumpernickel bread sandwich – Col could not recall what was on the sandwich except for lettuce and mayonnaise plus some kind of meat, probably lunchmeat – and the gentleman looking for work sat on their front porch and ate the sandwich, drank a glass of water or milk, and thanked his grandma profusely, before he wandered on down the street. He wasn't sure the guy was a "hobo", but he was a guy in need.

There were also "weekend wanderings" on some of the trails of the state park properties visited. The objective was to find your way back home.

Regarding these wanderings, Colton indicated that some memories exist, while some are surely camouflaged as "truth". I'm guessing, as your narrator, that some were dreams thought to have certainly been true in someone's life at some time in history, just not in Colton's.

The farthest he recalled they might have ventured was Clifty Falls State Park, down near Madison on the Ohio River. Then there was Spring Mill and the Grissom Memorial (after the unfortunate Apollo One disaster). McCormick's Creek – there was a cave there. (He is pretty sure that was Wolf Cave.) Turkey Run had bridges, ladders, small waterfalls, and great trails. Not far from Turkey Run was Shades State Park and also the Pine Hills Nature Preserve (not a "state park" but a cool place to hike). Then there was Brown County, probably the closest park to where he and his friends lived and the largest in the state, but not the most frequently visited. As he put on years, though,

Shades became his favorite park. Fewer people and great trails. More ladders. And stairs.

One particular aspect of Shades he talked about was following the trails in the summer when the grass and wild plants were high. With the little curve in the narrow trail, especially along the small creek, he could stop and look back and not be able to see where the trail came from. He had to back-track to figure that out. There was also the chance he couldn't see over the tall grass and natural vegetation. (And he had nearly maxed out on height by then.)

He remembered taking his younger daughter to Shades at least ten times, and likely more. Just the two of them hiking the trails. There was one, in particular, they always hiked – Trail 2 – which included a relatively simple outbound trail, aside from all the stairs (going down from that direction) about halfway through the trail near Sugar Creek. The return from the creek was quite rewarding to accomplish and followed a much smaller creek through a ravine. The map described Trail 2 as "rugged and very rugged". It was quite a trail for Indiana.

Colt once took both of his daughters together to Trail 2 at Shades. That was in the winter. The creek they could wander through on the trail that they loved in the summer was frozen solid, meaning that they spent that trip trying not to slip and fall. None of them fell. Fun times …

Now then, one fact of importance to note, all hikes up to this point were day hikes. No camping. No tents. No sleeping bags. Colton would leave in the morning from his home and be back in the evening, usually before dark – and that was without the benefit of Daylight Savings Time (DST), as they were in Indiana.

Note: DST was a distraction from the primary story for Colt. He mentioned that the biggest cities in the two states that, at the time, did not practice DST had the same newspaper publisher, and he thought that was the reason for DST being ignored. (I, the storyteller, mentioned to him that there was a third state.) Col thought that the publishers and employees of the newspapers vacationed there. What was truth and what wasn't seemed to be getting stretched a tad here.

Along with all this Hiking Business came snakes. Lots of snakes.

Col never saw a snake at Shades. He could not explain why he didn't care much for the creatures, but he just didn't. The first snake he saw, except in pictures, was along a trail by a creek or stream or river at McCormick's Creek State Park. (I suggested to Colton that the stream was likely McCormick's Creek – he insisted on the more blurred description of creek or stream or river …) The snake was black. And it was a pretty good-sized one. Could have been considered to be a big one. It was curled up, looking up at him. It didn't strike. And it didn't move. Not sure what kind of snake it was.

He did recall a girl in the group happened to warn him about the snake. Why the warning? He didn't know. Heck, it didn't really matter, did it? He thought the girl had saved his life. That could possibly be an overstatement or amplified opinion, but he did live to see another day.

When was the next big snake Col recalled seeing "in the wild"? He was in his late 60's. It was a Western Diamondback Rattlesnake near Mesa, Arizona. He said he was walking – no, hiking – with his friend, Tom, and they had left one of the trailheads from Hawes Trail to go back to Tom's place when they saw the snake in the road. It was just lying in the road, right in a residential area near Tom's place. Looked dead.

So, Tom, who had a walking stick, decided to go poke the dead snake. But as he approached, the snake flicked its tongue. Not dead …

They backed off a bit and, after a short time, the snake slithered off the road into the rocky terrain. Beautiful tail. Several rattles.

The next large snake Colton saw "in the wild" wasn't too long after that in Brown County. Once again, he wasn't sure what kind of snake – it was black in color, at least in part, with a pattern around its body that was somewhat lighter. It was wandering through the groundcover near one of the lakes in the state park. The creature was fairly fast-moving and fortunately, going away from them. He wasn't sure his dogs knew what it was or wasn't, but they wanted to check out the disturbance in the ground cover. Could be a short squirrel, they were probably thinking. Or a chipmunk. *No. Let the critter be.* (Note how he got the dogs into the story …)

There are a lot of black snakes – rat snakes are common, but in the park, it could have been a timber rattler. Looking up a photo later at home, the pattern was more akin to a timber rattlesnake than a rat snake, in his non-expert opinion. More dramatic for his story, if so. Colton did recall sometime later seeing a black rat snake in the downtown area of Nashville, Indiana, near the state park. It was making its way across an intersection, and traffic stopped for it. *Respect the snakes. They all talk with each other, don't they?*

Colt's also seen smaller snakes along his timeline of life, even in "the city". Actually, in several cities along that line. He once took one of his daughters to a science museum in Lansing (Michigan) where they happened to have a presentation on snakes that day. The presenter said that there was likely a snake in every yard in the city of Lansing. Every single yard! Colton went home and poked around – but he never saw a snake.

As retirement crept in on Colton, there were more non-venomous snakes seen living in Indianapolis (garter snakes) and then Brown County, Indiana (garter, worm snakes, ring neck, rat snakes, milk snakes). Not sure "the city" counts as "in the wild". The ones around his place at the edge of the woods of Brown County, however, would definitely count. The non-snake lover moved to the country where there were known to be a lot of snakes. Smart. Very smart … but that's our boy …

Colt did mention a couple of more stories about snakes that seemed worthy of inclusion. For example, he happened to find a snakeskin in his wood pile at his place in Brown County. It was under a plastic cover over the wood that he would burn in his wood stove. He expressed gladness that the snake had left the wood stack. And then, he found a snakeskin hanging from the trim around the top of the log part of his cabin … but wait for it … he found said skin INSIDE the cabin. It was sticking out from a small gap where he occasionally would see stuff on the windowsill below. He didn't immediately abandon the cabin. (As the storyteller, I wish I could have been able to get him to better articulate in words the finding of the snakeskin inside the cabin, but he would have this weird kind of shivering shake and would change the subject, so I let him off the hook.)

One final note on the subject … despite his fear of or dislike of snakes, Colton has never killed one. Of course, killing one is difficult while running away from them …

Chapter Four

Caves Small and Big, Hills Small and Mountains Big

And there were other "firsts" on these hiking adventures in the parks back in the days of Colton's youth …

First cave Col ever saw and entered in his life was on one of those hikes. That cave was at the same park as the first snake – McCormick's Creek. Wolf Cave, as noted earlier. The cave wasn't a big one. There were no unexplored rooms or tunnels. There were no cave paintings from years ago or graffiti from days ago. The space was tight. But most anyone could walk through it, part way, and then shimmy along the sides (to keep their feet dry from the water that sometimes collected) before giving up and crawling.

The cave was a little cooler, as you would expect. And there was a wetness, but it wasn't overwhelming. Not slimy, at least. Col thought the cave was actually dusty in spots, which could be a false memory. There was the faintest echo in the middle – but with all the frivolity of the hiking crew, Colton wasn't sure they would have heard insects or other critters or any other natural sounds.

It never seemed to be completely dark, but darker than outside for sure, and the flashlight beams of the fortuitous hikers somewhat prepared for their adventure danced along the walls, the ceiling, and the floor. There were no bones or bodies, but there may have been spiders. Colton did not know whether or not there were snakes. But surely, he would have remembered if there were. So, more than likely, there were no snakes in the cave – at least when he went through.

Technically and by its name – Wolf Cave – that was a cave. Col now thought it was just a partially underground path through rock. But I guess that qualifies as a "cave", doesn't it? Caves might be usually thought of as larger than what Wolf Cave was, but "large" is rather subjective as a value. The experts on these matters might have more thoughts to add here, but this really is not a guide on the definition of caves. One truth, though, that's worth mentioning here: Things change in perception from youth to adult.

Many years later, Colton decided to take his dogs for a walk in the park and chose the trail that looked – on the map – to be the best for them. Not too much mud or water made it ideal. It seemed to stay out of creek crossings and such. It ended up, though, that it went right past the same cave. With water and streams being the focus of his initial review of the map, he had missed noticing the cave was there too. He blew right by it. Wolf Cave was there, though.

Kids were in the cavern, going through it and playing. It appeared as if they were having great fun. And the dogs thought there was way too much excitement about a hole in the side of the hill.

Other dog owners must have looked for the same "clean" trail. Col says they must have passed a dozen dogs, including a few at the cave. (I'll quit pointing out the dogs making it into the story again – you may get tired of that…)

Compared to his remembrance of the cave from years prior, Colt thought the whole thing was not quite as obvious back then. He recalled it being off the trail just a bit farther. And with less fanfare. Possibly a sign and that was all? But he wasn't even sure about there being a sign. Maybe now there was more to be made of the cave. Regardless, he definitely did not remember benches where people could sit facing the cave entrance, probably for parents letting kids explore, looking for the wolf. And, he definitely did not remember how clear the area leading to the cave was – and the railings and all around it. And then the entrance – or exit? – on the other side was highlighted as well. Yes, this was now an attraction. Evidently, a big one. By the way, he didn't see a wolf.

Colton ended up liking caves and visited a bunch over the years. Most, if not all, did not permit random wandering by guests, but there was always the opportunity to walk or hike nearby – at least from a parking lot.

There was a cave in Spring Mill State Park that had a boat ride. That was different. More water than Wolf Cave, for sure. He thinks he once rode that boat years ago.

He talked about Mammoth Cave and seemed to think that might have been visited with the same bunch of friends who went there once when they were a little older, too, when he was in his early twenties. Or possibly, that was a trip he took with his first wife. He could not recall any longer. Too many sleeps since then.

There were also caves he visited in southern Indiana, Tennessee, Kentucky, Wisconsin, Missouri, and other states that he explored to the extent he could over the years, and he always took the tours. He was a sucker for tours.

What did he remember about all the tours that made the greatest impression? When they shut off the lights deep in the caverns. That was a darkness he could not reproduce elsewhere, like in his bedroom under the sheets. And blankets. And comforters. It was dark. Completely dark.

He remembered specifically the tour guide having the lights cut at Mammoth Cave (or so he thinks that's where it was). You could not see your hand in front of your face (wherever your hand or face were).

The little cave at McCormick's Creek did not compare at all to the blackness at Mammoth Cave, but in the middle of the crevice, while he was trying to avoid the water under his feet, there may have been very little light. The details were murky, maybe because there wasn't much light, and someone seemed to have a flashlight shining through the crevice, which pretty much defeated the darkness test.

As noted above somewhere, most caves were not open to general hiking or wandering. Some were with permits, and some were just open caverns. For the hiking enthusiast, seems more likely that one would find solace in parks and such versus underground caverns, leaving those to the spelunkers. Besides, the trails out in the open are filled with beauty and wonder for the hikers.

It does seem to be amazing that the trails of his youth seemed to shrink as he went up in years. But that wasn't always exactly true. Sometimes, they appeared to get even longer. In a certain regard, everything seemed smaller now, some sixty to seventy years later, but the distances weren't shorter. Kind of like a huge backyard for a child, complete with so much to explore and always and forever full of new adventures, becomes a thirty-minute (or less) mowing necessity as an adult, without a thrilling highlight reel.

Col also recalled the immensity of the "mountains" in the southern part of his home state. Or hills, if you will. He was a kid. But, even as a young adult, they were definitely bigger than the bridges over the interstate. And you would see one that stood out, higher than the surrounding land, including all the other hills. Said giant hill would be in front or to the side of you, and then, the next thing you knew, you were by it. The "mountain" was in the rearview mirror. Gone. Well passed. Quickly.

And then Colt visited Colorado ...

Now, he was in his middle to late twenties the first time he went there. The road had been relatively flat coming out of Nebraska heading toward Rocky Mountain National Park. After Greeley or, possibly, past Loveland – he could not recall any longer – there was this "hill" out in the distance. A "hill". And, relative to those "mountains" in his home state, which we just discussed, he assumed he would be past the hill, momentarily.

Any time, and he would be past it. Coming up any minute. Any time now. Yes. But no. No. For the longest time, the "hill" just wasn't going away. In fact, the "hill" started growing. Or so that's what it appeared to be doing. Slowly at first. And then still growing …

For that time – he thought thirty minutes or so – the insanely huge outcropping from the earth was still there. He wasn't in Brown County anymore. And he had come to realize he wasn't going to pass that thing momentarily.

Chapter Five

An Introduction to "Hiking" in the Woods

And so, there was a mental transformation, a reassignment of sorts regarding Colt's definition of 'hills'. Beauty, though, resides everywhere, and one need only to look. The reassignment, then, was in relative terms, where "different" didn't mean better or worse … just different. Like the line in gym class, there were tall participants in the land, and taller-still participants.

Before the much larger hills (or mountains), there was a canyon or whatever it might be called where the Big Thompson River flowed through. And there was Col and the river at the bottom of said canyon with warning signs about climbing to safety in the event of a flash flood.

This was serious stuff. There were certainly no signs like that between the hills back home.

The climb here would not be a snap, either – there were fairly steep rock walls. On both sides. And there was the initial concern for a shorter person of even getting over the guard rail to begin …

Every now and then, the road would go somewhat higher, and there would be the river below to one side or the other, with a mountain on the opposite side. Then you'd be back with mountains on both sides, driving right beside the water.

Homes were sometimes built up higher on the wall of rock. Perhaps their owners hoped to be high enough to be safe in the event of a flood. Others, obviously the risk takers, were essentially by the water, with a nice setting … until a flood. Regardless, that was quite the road. Beautiful. Scenic.

Then, you popped out approaching Estes Park. Shops and cars and people – oh, my – and motels and restaurants, and a hotel with a rather shining history (as in, "all work and no play makes Jack a dull boy").

The town Estes Park was located east of one of the entrances to Rocky Mountain National Park. Once in the park, the purchasing, lodging, and eating options were far fewer. Civilization was in the town. Nature was in the park. Not much in the way of "mixing it up" in either one. You were basically in civilization, or you were in nature.

Colton remembered driving the main road up to a visitor's center, then to the Continental Divide, and – eventually – to a town on the western side of the mountains and the park. There was a big lake there, too. And then, they came back. It was uphill, he said, at least part of both directions. There seemed to be fewer barriers, as he recalls, and so they could stop here and there and wander out into the wild. He learned rather fast that running up a hill was a tad different at that elevation. Let's just say that to saunter was easier. There was a perception that the air was thinner.

He participated in no major hikes on that first journey west. Oh, there were some jaunts. The longest trek was around Bear Lake, he figured, and other trails in that general area of the park. That was at a lower altitude than up above the tree line, although it was still way higher than back home. More people out for an excursion were found there at the lower altitude, too. The area was beautiful. And he didn't remember any snakes or caves.

He told me he didn't want to take what he called the scenic route at the park – a one-lane road, Old Fall River Road, that was only open part of the year and only one way, which was up. He wasn't sure where that dirt road would take him, and he wasn't much for surprises.

He also didn't take any of the "real" trails (excluding those around Bear Lake). The official ones. The monsters. Oh, sure – they didn't look too bad at the trailheads near the parking areas, but they disappeared into the wild, over another hill, around rocks, past shrubs and lower growth, to commune with nature. Yeah, he could have chosen to hike these trails and talk to trees. And possibly mountain lions or other large beasts with the capability of making his day more exciting than he preferred. He wasn't sure about snakes as he thought they would not be at high elevations. But he also wasn't sure why he thought that.

He was not prepared for anything too exciting or ambitious this first trip to the giant hills. He didn't even have drinking water…

Colton says he has been back to Rocky Mountain National Park several times since that first eye opening drive in from Loveland. The last time was a few years ago. That time, he was surprised to run into snow on the side of the road near the visitor's center, up Trail Ridge Road. And the snow was falling, too. Turns out, the center was not yet completely open for the year. The next day, case in point, the road was closed due to the ~~new~~ snow. And that was late June!

After visiting the Rockies, Col's vision about hiking changed, a bunch. He seemed satisfied with shorter day trips. Oh, there was chatter about The Appalachian Trail – the younger of his daughters was really interested in that adventure. For a time. Not forever. During that interested period, however, he and that one daughter and her mom (one of his ex's – none ever lived in Texas) were up in New Hampshire, and they passed a sign for The Trail. She was psyched about it and had to check it out. They dropped her mom at the hotel and went back.

Colt said they stopped at a trailhead parking lot. They got out and wandered south on part of The Trail, her dream. They walked – no, hiked – about a mile or a little more and ran into a hiker headed north (his beard was really long.), back towards where Colton and his daughter had parked. The hiker had two hiking poles and, as Colton told the story, they weren't those finely crafted metal ones, but were wooden ones and fairly tall, above his head anyway. The guy had a pack on his back that was literally huge. There were things hanging from it, possibly for easy access to something.

Col's guess was that he had been out there somewhat longer than the time that he and his daughter had been there. But there was no interview of said hiker to get any big questions answered – like the obvious: *How long have you been out here?* – or any other stimulating inquiry. Colton said they merely small talked. Very small talk.

On the subject of small talk, Colton thought that happened too often. Instead of the great query, there was the more typical (and useless) "How about this weather?" or "How about them Colts?" Lame. That's what it was, he claimed, lame.

Nevertheless, the hiker chatted with them for a couple of minutes or so, politely. He then continued on. The two day-hikers and horrible interviewers went on their way, but not for too much longer, maybe a mile or so down The Trail. Colton did not recall if his daughter had any impression of The Trail or anything else about the experience.

Colt told me that a few weeks later he was at home watching an evening news show. The show had one of those human-interest stories that was near the end of the half hour. The story was about a guy who had just completed The Appalachian Trail for about his seventh time.

"THAT'S HIM!" Colt's daughter exclaimed.

"Who?" Colton asked.

"The guy we met on The Appalachian Trail!"

And that was him. And he was doing a real interview. With good questions. Intriguing ones. No weather questions …

Colt and his daughter never did "the big trail". Oh, I suppose they still could someday before he's eighty. Or ninety. That leaves them some time for planning, wouldn't you say?

I guess his daughter maintained the dream for a bit, but then the objective faded. Life moved on. Or perhaps she remembered the backpack on that hiker. It sure looked heavy.

Chapter Six

The Goal Begins to Emerge

And so, Col moved on. He became busy in his career. Too busy. Way too busy. Oh, he occasionally wandered out to a park or trail, but far less frequently than in his past. His daughter went to college (with a smaller backpack). And life for everyone in his circle was centered on achieving their own goals, hopes, and dreams. Or at least moving along some sort of path forward.

Colt could have taken a long walk in the woods, but, no, he did not …

Work took over, pretty much. (He doesn't recommend that approach to life – due to the whole we've only one life to live thing…) There wasn't a lot of time to even do much day-hiking, let alone a week or a month or even longer jaunts. Colton did walk. He walked a ton – well, a short ton. In other words, he walked some. He actually had a pretty good step count for a desk jockey, but there was no threat of any record being broken by his efforts. That said, the "walking" we're discussing here was not the same as "walking" in the woods. But at least he was doing something to keep his legs limber.

There was no camping. He didn't seem to find time, and even if he had, he didn't have any experience in that activity, anyway. Most of his backyards were also too open for a tent. It would stand out. There was one that had plenty of trees, but most of them were smaller and spaced out. Col told me that he had thirteen different kinds of trees in that particular yard, one of each of several different kinds.

During this phase of increased work involvement, which stretched over several years and a couple of marriages, another sporting opportunity arose, though. Well … it sadly arose. Bowling. It didn't require driving very far, and it was done in a relatively short period of time. He wasn't awful, but he wasn't going to bowl a perfect game either, let alone win any money. He had bowled off and on for years. He had an IU bowling ball – cream and crimson. A 14 to 15-pounder, he thought. (He still has the ball, but he wouldn't weigh the thing for me for this story.)

I noted that the attention he received when he was on a bowling league – still work-related – created a bubble of excitement from him. Briefly. He went on and on about how there was always a bunch of people wandering over from other teams when he was bowling. And he liked that. But the bubble burst when he finally realized and then accepted that the faux attention paid to him was merely to spend time with his teammates in the mixed league – three, rather pretty, young ladies. When they were not bowling, the guests chatted with the ladies and really could not have cared less about Colton's bowling prowess.

That recollection also reminded Colt of one of his big wins on bowling night. One evening, his wife and younger daughter, the prospective hiker, dropped by the alley. They explained they had had an accident. His response was to ask if they were all right. Many males would have asked about the car. But not Colton! No, he did good, as some would say, including the three young ladies on his team. And here it was April Fool's Day when this happened, but Colton was no fool that day!

Colton was asked to participate in a men's league. His brother-in-law asked him. Once. And it wasn't work-related. So that was good. But the men in men's leagues get more serious – basically, it appears to be the Super Bowl of Bowling every single week, every single game, every single frame. If the teammates and competitors drank enough beer, however, the intensity seemed to fall off somewhere in the second game … that, or they became so angry with their own performance, they didn't notice yours quite as much.

Colton mentioned that he seemed to have this weird thing about bowling – if he had not bowled for some time, say three to six months, for example, the first time he would bowl, he would be good. Sometimes very good. Then the thinking kicked in, and he became the usual average bowler he most of the time was. And boy did that matter the first week, which is when they set your handicap. So, Week 1, he rolls his first 600-plus series in his life (all three games over 200). Week 2? He drops to a 165 or less average per game. Despite his relative consistency after that of around 165 or so, after a dip to the 140's, he was treated as a right fielder … again… and that didn't wear off for a bunch of weeks, if it ever did, at all.

For some reason, he was not asked again to carry the ball into battle on the oiled lanes and avoid the gutters of truth. One time. One men's league. That was it. No thrill of victory, just agony … lots of agony.

He had been "off of the lanes" for some time. Years. Colt had moved on. Forgotten about all that. Still had his IU bowling ball, but he really, very seriously, threw himself into his work to get out of that right field feeling (no offense, he says, to true right fielders…). He was attending a meeting of an industry committee, as he remembered it – wasn't sure which meeting or what committee – but he recalled sitting in one of those lobby bars at the hotel where they were meeting. He thought it was in New York City somewhere, but could not quite confirm that. Could have been any one of several cities. He had worked for over thirty years in the life insurance industry with a focus on underwriting and risk selection. He was taking more of an industry role, in addition to his company role, taking on committee assignments and positions of responsibility. He was busier. And that kept him from trying any new sports – which was a big plus.

Lobby bars at large hotels were not really traditional bars. No wooden stools, but instead, much more comfortable chairs. They tended to be well lit. Open versus cramped. No big screen TVs, and rarely smaller ones. They were relatively quiet with muted conversations. The occasional exception was a group of co-workers gathering their nerve to head out into whichever big city they were in.

As life would have it, Colton was chatting in one of these lobby establishments. He seemed to always be chatting (at least with people he knew pretty well or shared a strong, common interest with). It was he and one other guy. On this occasion, they had chatted enough about work and somewhere during the conversation, the topic changed to hiking. And then camping was added. Turns out that Colt's friend, who he had known for at least a couple or three years or more, was an avid hiker, camper, and technical climber. Colt, at that time, didn't know which end was up on a backpack. And here was an expert. He was learning more about his friend – this was all new news to Col. And it was good news, as he did like learning about people's interests. His memory may have been lousy at recalling said interests later, but learning was fascinating to him.

Col mentioned that he had never camped in his life and had only done day-hikes, but he thought camping might be interesting and something that he might try some time. His friend, Bill, told him he should try it. "Live a little – camp in the woods," he said.

And then Col said those fateful words, "Maybe before I turn age 60, it would be a good personal goal to get out in the wild and camp."

"When will that be?" Bill asked.

"Oh, three and a half years. That should give me time to get the guts to do the camping and get the stuff I would need to accomplish that," Col replied.

"If you don't," Bill responded, "you would be missing out on an incredible experience."

Bill and Colt agreed to work on avoiding the missing of that opportunity. And there was plenty of time to get that done, if before his sixtieth birthday remained the objective. As you know, Colt didn't really have many goals, if any, so having one kind of stood out for him – like a sore thumb.

A goal was actually being considered.

A goal might have been being formed.

It was not yet clearly established.

And it was materializing for a guy who had never even slept in a tent in his own backyard. In the city. Come to think of it, he had never slept in a living room tent made with a sheet over chairs or however one did that.

Keep in mind that Bill was also not talking about camping in a living room or backyard, either.

The clock was ticking faster than the planning, for sure. But then there was another industry meeting. And within a year, or thereabouts, of that very first discussion between two friends, once again, Bill and Col both attended a meeting and got together in the hotel lobby bar, to chat.

"So, how's the camping plans going?" Bill asked.

"Well, I haven't totally forgotten about the idea," Col said.

Truth told, he continued to have thoughts about it, but only as a dream. There was no plan. Nothing even close to one.

"Incredible experiences await," Bill claimed.

After the meeting, Colt became his usual busy self, setting aside the potential exploit of camping. He was too busy or something.

Then, there was yet another meeting. And yet another a year later or at least a few months later. In another city. Both guys were there, once again. Col was still his pathetic, hackneyed, predictable, dull, unoriginal, tired, vapid, half-baked, banal, unimaginative, stale, boring, lifeless, hoary, hollow, uninspiring self. Awful, really. Bill was out there climbing – mountain climbing – in the Cascades, Olympics, and elsewhere. Scaling peaks, seeing the sights, wandering around in woods. He was camping. Col hadn't even tried a living room "tent" to gain any "experience".

And then, again … another year went by. Colton was running out of time, and people were running out of adjectives to describe his tiresome self. He had about eight or so months left, as he recollected, to accomplish this passive dream and flickering goal.

But then, something happened – Bill might have laid out the timeline or called for a "new Colton". A challenge was tendered. At last, Bill and Colton agreed on a week or two, starting toward the middle of July that year, running into the first week of August, about five months before Colt's sixtieth birthday, that used to be three or four years away. Two months or so away then was all that was left before the hiking and camping experiment commenced.

Time flies, doesn't it?

The simplistic description of the deal was this: Col would meet Bill in Seattle, where Bill lived, and they would wander out to do some camping in the woods … somewhere.

Now, this was getting real. Col couldn't just go in a house if a coyote howled in the distance, and there were coyotes reported near the river running through his neighborhood. Also note that his backyard had no fences.

And there he was also the issue that he had no equipment, no knowledge, and no experience. All he had was a goal (his only real goal) and a dream.

Bill provided a list of things Col needed. Col had nothing on that list. (Correction, he did have a sleeping bag. Yeah, it was only one thing, but it was a start.) Realizing his predicament, Bill offered to provide some of the requirements, so the list diminished a little. Well actually, the list greatly diminished.

Backpack and toilet paper – that's all that was left to obtain.

Col didn't ask a lot of questions about the toilet paper. He did, however, get recommendations on backpack brands and such. A backpack was purchased – he could not remember from where. It was a nice green one. Dark green. Metal frame, but lightweight. He could take it apart to fit in his suitcase better – luckily as he hadn't considered the size and the packing of the pack until he had already arrived home with the purchase). It was a rather tall backpack – seemed like a lot of stuff could get into that thing, making it heavy. Real heavy. A flashback to the guy on the Appalachian Trail may have occurred. Anyway, Col had plenty of toilet paper at home – so he was then done on both items one and two. His sleeping bag was recovered from his basement storage, and it didn't smell too musty. Reservations for flights were made.

He was ready ... sort of ...

Everett Kunzelman

Chapter Seven

The Evolving Details – Seattle Perspective

Colton hadn't even asked where they were going to hike and camp, so all options were available. *Just let Bill make the decision and go with his plan,* Colton coached himself. He figured Bill would tell him where they were off to when he made it to Seattle. Or on the way to wherever they were going. Or at the trailhead itself.

Not asking in advance about some of the details was kind of Colton-esque (a word you may see again). He had done pretty well in his career by doing at least some degree of planning, but he sometimes failed at that on a personal level. And since this trip was a mix of business and personal, with a witness, there was a little pressure for the old man. It wasn't just business, even though he would be traveling with someone in the same type of business he was in. This trip, they would have plenty of time to get to know each other on a more personal level than Colton was used to.

Bill must have been thinking, *"Where can I take the old man out here in the wild?"*

Colton was almost 60, although he didn't really look like he was ready for a walker. Not even a cane. Yet, Bill was younger. The good news for Bill, though, was that Colton claimed to be in very good health. He had all his original parts (appendix, tonsils, joints, and so forth), no serious ailments, and no arthritis or other joint issues limiting his mobility. There was his thumb issue, but that was not (yet) a huge irritant in his life. While Colton might not be one to just take off up a hill at full speed, perhaps his general well-being would make for a steady performance.

Bill knew Col was not trained in the technical aspects, but those were not expected to come into play during their excursion. That was the only real restriction Col placed on Bill – there were to be no technical climbing requirements for the event.

Bill seemed to spend a lot of time in the Cascades. There were a lot of possibilities along the seven hundred or so miles of the range, including Mount Rainier, but the Cascades might be a little bit much, at least the sections where Bill and his friends liked to go. Mount Rainier was definitely out of the question. Bill wondered whether Colton had at least seen Rainier from a plane as he had been to Seattle at least once. The travel to the Cascades would likely be longer than to, say, the Olympics.

Plus, the Cascades might be too much for one who hasn't even opened a tent and slept in it.

A real beginner … that was Colton.

Bill, for the reasons stated, later explained that he thought the Cascades were definitely out of the question. He was hopeful of finding something acceptable in the Olympics. The Olympics also had interesting roads and so forth to get out there, adding to the overall adventure. There was a floating bridge and the ferry. Exciting, perhaps, for a newby. Even the return trip from the opposite direction would be cool, if Colton were still conscious.

Bill later told me (your narrator) that, at the time, he also wondered if Colton had ever been in a helicopter? If he had not – and if he ended up unconscious from the Olympic journey – then that would be another new experience. Oh, he might have to be told about it after the fact, but yes, he just might get his first helicopter ride out of the adventure, too.

The Olympic Mountains had numerous options that would likely not require dragging an old person out of the trees after his failure to thrive at serious hiking and camping. Or that's what Bill perceived. Or hoped for, at any rate. There was, of course, the hope that he didn't fall down any mountain – the snow in late July and early August should not be so bad that he could slip. Of course, there was always the slim chance of him having to drag Colt out – and thus, the Olympics would be easier for that in some areas as well. *Do I know how to build a sled to drag him,* he wondered?

With all this in mind, Bill took a look at the Olympic Mountain area as the setting for Colt's attempt at making his goal.

Recall that Bill has been described as a well-qualified, mountain person. And he was – still is. Not one of those over-grown bearded, scruffy-looking guys out of the woods. He was a white-collar employee of a big company, but he had the skills of a person who could do other things in life, and potentially make a living doing them. Bill could be leading tours of hiking and camping in the wild. He was an expert of sorts – definitely when compared to the rookie, Colton. He had to consider Colt's experience – rather his lack of experience – and find the sort of adventure that was survivable. Survive and walk out on his own – that was his plan for Colt.

Where to go … where to go …?

Since Colton was arriving in the earlier part of the day, there was time to head out and possibly even get in a reasonably good hike before that first camping experience. There had to be enough to give Colton a taste of the hike and yet have time to get his tent up before dark. Bill did not want to be doing a lot after dark, except sleeping.

Made sense, right?

So, what were the options?

One that jumped to Bill's mind immediately was one that included Deer Park, Cameron Creek, Grand Pass, Obstruction Point, and Grand Valley, along with other creeks, mountains, and trails. That was all farther west, though, and required a longer travel time to arrive and more moderate hiking for a rookie, but it would likely be a lot busier, with potentially many more people. More people meant more assistance in dragging said rookie out if need be. But no, Bill wanted to be positive in his planning approach. Positive in the sense that he wanted to give Colt a great introduction to the wild. So, while being a wonderful opportunity for safety considerations, a large crowd might not be the introduction Bill was looking for. After all, "out there in the wild" did not mean walking on a busy path with lots of "excuse me" moments. They needed a lonesome path. A truly wild path. Beautiful sights.

There was Upper Big Quilcene Trailhead. They had to start somewhere where they could park the car. So that was one option. The Upper Big Quilcene Trail, from that trailhead, was almost seven miles to where they could take the Upper Dungeness Trail and onto the Constance Pass Trail via the Home Lake Trail. Good choices … and it was a good option to include Constance Pass. There were also several campsites along the Upper Big Quilcene, meaning they could be faster or slower along the first seven miles and still get somewhere that had a semblance of a camping site before darkness came. Might be other people there or not, but the site would look like a primitive camp, and offer a decent potential sleeping site.

Bill did not want to scare the man to death on his first experience by truly hanging out wherever they might stop in the woods, or what was known as "boondocking". They could always do that later in the experience, like for Night Two. Or Night Three. Whenever else was fine … just not Night One.

Mount Townsend Trailhead didn't offer as many alternative routes as others, so Bill kind of ruled that one out. Essentially, he had one nice trail to access, other options just didn't come much into play as quickly as he might have desired, considering the rookie he'd have with him. There was climbing the peak as a possibility. *But yeah, let's not scale a peak on Hike Number One.*

The Little Quilcene Trailhead presented a route leading to the Tubal Cain Trail or the Gold Creek Trail (a turn right or left sort of thing). The Tubal Cain might be best, but led to Marmot Pass, which meant they might as well do the first one (Upper Big Quilcene Trailhead), which ends up through that same passage in the mountains. It was a cool area.

Then there was the Upper Dungeness Trailhead. If they stopped at the store (that would be Longhouse Market), that was the best place to start and then they could proceed to Constance Pass, and very likely points beyond, and come back down by Royal Creek. Maybe. There were side trails and way trails (kind of underdeveloped or undermaintained ones) all along this route with a relatively easy camp to make the first night before dark. *That would really work as one route to seriously consider.* Getting to Royal Creek from the west or after Constance Pass would be a tough call, one that depended on the weather and any remaining snow. There were pathways over to Royal Creek that would not really involve any technical expertise – and this was not going to be a time to provide that training.

"Next, Colton, add a friction hitch to the rope…"

No … there would be no conversations of that kind on this trip.

Upper Big Quilcene or Upper Dungeness?

Both good choices.

Longhouse Market – a must see for a city boy – was best seen on one of the ways to a trailhead. Now there were other trailheads that direction farther west from the Market, but the views around Constance Pass were near perfect, so all Bill's thoughts seemed to head that way.

Bill knew the area very well. And he wasn't planning for the need to drag his older friend out of the woods. Although, it was somewhat funny to think about. He wondered if he could find a book entitled, "How to Build a Rescue Sled" and place it on the car seat or in his living room when Colt arrived. Might be cruel. Might get a laugh. Could be an instructional read, though … just saying.

Upper Dungeness Trailhead won as the chosen destination!

Bill would surprise Colton with the news when he arrived.

A couple of weeks before the show got under way, Bill acquired the permits and made the plans he needed to make (Colt thought there might be permits required, but he didn't know for sure. He was the rookie, after all.) Bill? Well … Bill was ready ... ready for anything that was about to happen.

56

Chapter Eight

"Pack Toilet Paper"

There were thoughts that popped up as Colt was making his preparations for the camping extravaganza. Oh, so many thoughts.

There was a recollection in his old memory banks of someone he knew in his life who once noted that "camping" would be staying in a lower-level Marriott than a JW Marriott. Col's idea of "camping" had some obscurity due to his complete lack of experience, but at least his notion wasn't that of a hotel room (even a less expensive one, even a non-Marriott, or a motel with any number in its name).

His "goal" or thought or curiosity of years gone by was to camp "out in the wild". Was that ever a goal before he was approached by Bill in a hotel lobby bar? The timetable "before he reached the age of 60" had definitely become part of the equation. And now, there was money invested – a flight for starters – and the really big backpack – so this deal was getting a little more serious for Colton. He also owned a fair amount of toilet paper, but not as much as many people following the panic of the pandemic when store shelves were emptied. He didn't empty any store shelves or even fill a grocery cart with his toilet paper of choice. Humans …

His thoughts naturally went to reminiscing about all of his day-hikes. Hiking had been great for him and to him! He loved it! Indiana state park hikes were his primary equivalence. (Similitude might be the better descriptive term. "Equivalence" might draw too much on "equality" versus, say, a "similar" happening. Remember, I've been paid to find the right words to tell this epic adventure.)

The elevation changes on a hike near his home might be 500 feet in total – not really sure, could be half that. And it isn't all at once, either. He had driven up Trail Ridge Road in Rocky Mountain National Park. And there was a huge total elevation change there. But that was not the same as walking (or hiking) up that road. He recalled seeing bikers going up that road. It looked tough. That said, he had ridden his bike over interstate bridges and survived. But there was no biking on this journey with Bill, so that really didn't matter, he said.

Lacking any real understanding or factual knowledge of the coming adventure, worries did not set in for Colt. Ignorance was wonderfully blissful. He didn't even know where they were going, so there were no internet look-ups to install panic. Not at all. He was in complete and total ignorance. That isn't to say that

Bill didn't tell him where they were headed, but he didn't recall having been told.

Speaking of the bliss of ignorance, a couple of weeks before his flight, the reality hit Colton that he really didn't have good hiking boots or shoes. He did own worn, "slightly used" sneakers or tennis shoes. While a little late to be thinking about footwear, he miraculously found a great pair of boots, and they were on sale at The Rack (in the store, not online). No, he did not have enough time to break them in. But he got very lucky – they were perfect!

As a side note: Colton said they were the best shoes he has ever had, before or since. Made by Ecco. They were boots about as high as high-top tennis shoes, maybe just a tad higher. Black. Water-repellant. Or resistant. Or waterproof. Not sure of the exact terminology to use. And he was still wearing them over ten years later. He hated to part with the boots, despite the wear on the heels. He did add that he finally bought a new pair, also Ecco, also black, but designed a little differently. He wears the new ones once in a great while, but he remains committed to the old ones that took the big hike with him.

Now we return to our story…

So, with the new shoes, the backpack, the toilet paper, and the sleeping bag, Colton was ready to go. He was getting a little excited … or was that anxiousness (as in anxiety)? It was something. There was something going on with him.

The flight to Seattle was in two parts. From where Colton was living during that point in his career and life, there were direct flights to few places considered "destinations". But there were plenty with layovers. That is not to suggest that those direct places to fly weren't wonderful places to visit, but you could get to most of those by car, within a few hours.

There was always risk with connections. And Colt experienced a few glitches, let's say. So, his first flight was delayed. Not much, but enough to heighten his anxiety – it was more about the luggage transfer than about him getting to the gate. All he could do was hope the luggage made it. The toilet paper? He hoped that made it, too.

And that made him wonder, *why not just get toilet paper in Seattle?* They did have indoor plumbing out there. But the toilet paper had properly filled in the empty voids in his luggage. All he had in the biggest suitcase he owned was the backpack, along with his sleeping bag and some clothes for the return flight, plus a couple of changes of clothes for the hike. (We'll come back to that change of clothes for the hike later …)

The second leg of his flight was uneventful, though it was the longer of the two. Col got to thinking about Seattle. He had been there once that he remembered, over twenty years prior. And then he remembered a second time which was eight to ten years earlier for an insurance industry meeting. He had bought a sport coat at the original Nordstrom's in Downtown Seattle – he needed one for a meeting and hadn't packed one. He recalled watching fish being thrown at Pike's Place. (He did not participate. It was too much like a sport, and we know some stories by now about Colt and sports.) He had encouraged his staff to use the "fish principles" that Pike's taught for their workplace – choose your attitude, make your customer's day, be present, and have fun. He thought it was a good way to run a railroad, with or without the tossing of fish. Colt also thought those four principles were decent guidelines for living in general.

That first trip to Seattle years prior was in the month of May, around 1990. The first trip was also a business trip, but he stayed over a few days and went to Mount Rainier with a friend who had moved out there a couple of years or so earlier.

One thing he remembered was entering the park at Mount Rainier. His friend Dan was driving, and they had not gone too far past the entrance when they saw a little snow in a ditch. Colton wanted to take a picture – I mean, it was snow … in May! There's no snow in May that he'd ever seen. That was race time back home (as in Indy500 race time). Dan suggested he wait until they were closer to the Visitor's Center to get a "better picture" of the snow.

That's when the snow started getting even deeper – not a lot at first, but Dan was right – there would be even better pictures to be taken because there was definitely more snow!

And then it got even deeper.

And still deeper!

The road leading to the Visitor's Center on the last part of the drive was surrounded by snow about fourteen feet deep. In May! The road was carved through snow.

Such great pictures! Dan was right.

They could hear the snow-clearing work beyond the Center as they approached. Even though there was more snow than he had ever seen in his life, Colton said that he could still see Rainier.

It was a beautiful sight, he said.

The Visitor's Center was a typical one for a national park, according to Colt's limited experience. There were displays about the area, maps, even a presentation of the variability in topography in a three-dimensional model. There were rangers to answer questions. Restrooms. There might have been a giftshop – he could not say for sure on that either, but there likely was.

As they were poking around the Center, which was comfortably busy, they discovered these public service posters that were illustrating what you should and should not do while hiking and camping in the area. There was a camper/hiker they used to demonstrate a bunch of mistakes. His name was Colton. *Wonderful!* The posters screamed, "DON'T BE LIKE COLTON!"

His memory of things not to do had long since faded, but he had Bill, an expert, to guide and help him once in the Seattle area. He certainly didn't want to be a poster child this time around.

PART II

THE BIG EVENT
(Hiking and Camping in the Olympic Mountains)

64

Chapter Nine

Finally, Heading Toward the Wild

Colton arrived in Seattle. He was ready to spend several days, possibly even a week, could be longer, hiking and camping … somewhere. Bill was there to pick him up at the airport. Since it was early in the day there, given the even earlier flight from out east, there was plenty of time to head out for that first night of camping.

Bill was kind enough to loan Colt a few things he did not have for camping that he had thought of after he'd sent him the packing list. Toilet paper … Colt had remembered the toilet paper … and his sleeping bag. All was right with the world.

Toilet paper seemed to be very important, to Bill.

"Can't have too much," he said early on.

But looking at how much Col brought, Bill reconsidered. "Maybe we don't take all that."

After loading the backpack and hanging stuff off the pack, just like the guy on the Appalachian Trail years ago, the final product weighed roughly forty pounds. And that was without including a change of clothes. There was no room left. It was a huge backpack – in Colt's eyes – but still, it only held so much. There was a tent, sleeping bag, and all kinds of necessities Bill said he would need. He couldn't recall everything in there, but he did know they had decided to carry a water purifier. With the purifier, they did not have to carry water, reducing the weight significantly from what it could have been.

The preparations were for a maximum of seven nights. But that whole no-change-of-clothes thing still bothered the white-collar city boy – I mean, seven days in the same clothes? Food was expected to last that long. And there were no extras ... of anything. Colton was to carry some of the food – the energy bars and related delicacies. Bill, however, had most of it, although Colton didn't really know what was in his backpack.

"Can you tolerate gluten-free food?" Bill asked.

Colton thought a second and replied, "I'm not sure what that means. I've never had to restrict my diet in any way."

"Good," Bill noted. "You'll be fine. A few days with no gluten won't get you sick. Do you have IBS?"

"Some indication of that, but no special diet and such," Colton answered.

IBS is irritable bowel syndrome. The two guys, both with a lot of medical knowledge required for their jobs, knew the acronym. So many TLAs, so little time. ("TLA" stands for "three-letter acronym", in case you didn't know.)

"Then actually you may be better off without any gluten. All is well. No concern," Bill stated.

Guess there was always spear fishing if they were running short on vittles. Fish are gluten-free – at least Colt thought they were. Fresh red meat would be gluten free, wouldn't it? If they bagged a deer, for example. How they would "bag a deer" would be a huge question, but still. More possibilities could surface on the venture, Colt supposed. Having done zero research, since he didn't know where they were going, the size and number of possible wildlife was an unknown.

Back to clothes …

The old story Col had heard was that men could make underwear good for several days by wearing them inside out and backwards. What's that – four days? Just doing the math. Two directions (forward and then backward), then normal and inside out? (Colt claimed never to have done that himself prior to or since the big event.) So, for a period of seven days, that's not even twice in each "position". That's like not really wearing them entirely for two complete cycles. He didn't share his concerns about this with Bill, as he did not want to appear uneasy about that kind of thing.

The car was soon loaded up, and the boys took off for the ferry, encountering an average Seattle area traffic jam (or jams) that Bill found frustrating even after all of his years there. Having driven in Boston, Colton didn't think traffic was particularly horrible in Seattle. In an attempt to relieve Bill's angst, Colton shared a tale about his first left turn in Boston. The light had turned green, so he eased up. That's what he did at home in the Midwest, so that's what he did in Boston. But the two cars behind him in line just turned in front of the oncoming traffic. There seemed to be a slight pause by the traffic continuing straight from the other direction, but it wasn't a big deal to anyone other than Colton. In the Midwest, they would likely have been broadsided. Regardless, Seattle traffic seemed busy to Col, but not horrid, like Boston.

They did arrive at the ferry on time – the Bainbridge Island Ferry. Col could not recall how close they were to missing the boat. Literally. But, they didn't have to take a run at it, launching the car to then hopefully land on the boat ... like a *Dukes of Hazard* stunt.

The ferry, following the water path of Washington State Road 305, would haul their car and them and all the other cars and vehicles, plus people across the water a bit, landing or whatever nautical term was appropriate for arriving, near Winslow, Washington, on Bainbridge Island. In other words, across the bay. One of the bays. There were several.

The loudspeaker on the ferry advised them to watch for "pods of Orcas" But nope. There were none. Bill thought that the invitation was just to keep the passengers who did not know any better busy, essentially a story to make the trip more exciting than it really was. Bill also reminded Colton that this was

Washington, not Arizona, so there would be no standing on the corner watching for any flatbed Fords.

The Winslow port was located where just about all there was to see were the Olympic Mountains to the west. Although they did not see any submarines, there was a huge base south of their landing point several miles, the third largest naval base in the United States, according to the "fun facts" on the internet (if true). They did not see the aircraft carrier Nimitz either –which was presumably based there. Perhaps they were in stealth mode. The Enterprise was in "stealth mode" in one of the *Star Trek* movies when they "parked" in San Francisco. So that must be a thing, Col figured.

Off the ferry, they proceeded northwest on the land version of 305. It was drier and seemed to have more traditional definition, as in lanes and such. They passed the Bainbridge Island Museum of Art. Colton liked art, but there was no notation on the website of the museum having a Monet, so his interest dwindled. The art was primarily that of artists in the region, which was still valuable art with historical significance. Monet was not from the Puget Sound area, despite the Sound having a French connection, as it was named after one of the Huguenots or French protestants there in the 1700's. A Monet in the collection would be sort of appropriate with that French influence, don't you agree?

The route toward Olympic National Park and its surrounding properties took them past Liberty Bay. It made Colt think of Botany Bay, another *Star Trek* reference (as well as an Australian one). There were no apparent Augments noted, no criminal activities.

The camper-to-be and the experienced camper proceeded toward Agate Pass Bridge, on up State Route 305. Colt learned that the bridge was built around 1950 – his year of birth, he claimed – and was about a quarter mile across. It was a steel bridge. Bill thought there was a ferry there at one time – way before his time, him being young and all. (That really was not a dig at the older Colton. Just the facts, sir.)

After some twists and turns, here and there, from 305 to highway 3 then to 104, they were at the Hood Canal Floating Bridge on State Road 104. The real name is the William A. Bugge Bridge, named after a civil engineer who was instrumental in transportation projects across the Northwest and the West Coast. And that particular bridge was interesting. Colton had never been on a "floating bridge" that he could recall. He had been on a "singing" one in Indianapolis – the bridge over White River was a grate so tires "sung" driving across it. No floating one there, though. The Bugge Bridge was almost a mile and a half across. Bill said that it had been rebuilt once after a storm, taking almost three years to build originally and then another three years to rebuild. It opened somewhere near the middle to allow the occasional ship to pass through, but primarily to allow Trident submarines to move out of the base area further south. The "drawbridge effect" takes place with part of the bridge kind of rolling back over the approach on both sides to create the opening, versus rising like a more conventional drawbridge. There was no opening to occur that day. And Colton did not recall that the bridge "felt funny", moving or shifting or rolling or anything like that as it floated on the water. (Note: There were at least two other floating bridges in the Seattle area. They didn't take those, though.)

Colton explained to Bill that he did go over a drawbridge that lifted in western Michigan, near Grand Haven, over the Grand River, not too far from Lake Michigan. The bridge wasn't terribly long, and it was a steel grate bridge – yep, another singing variety. That bridge did rise in the middle, occasionally getting stuck, which left people with no alternative but to wait.

The road after the floating bridge took them west, without much fanfare, toward Blyn, kind of at the south end of the Sequim Bay, at which point it continues to Sequim, farther up the bay to the west. That general area of Washington along the northern coast of the Olympic Peninsula has the Olympic National Park and Olympic National Forest with various subsections, including a rainforest. That's the northwesternmost area of the lower forty-eight states. Vancouver Island, part of Canada, is across the strait from the peninsula.

While trying to figure out where he was, Colton learned that the name for the general area of water between Washington and the island had been renamed within the past couple of years prior to their visit as the Salish Sea. That did not help him a lot, but it was information, and he liked information, as you know.

They made a stop at the store – Longhouse Market – near Blyn. The Jamestown S'Kallam Tribe of indigenous people ran the store and many of the businesses along that stretch of road. Bill said he had always been impressed with them. Could be the Market itself that was impressive.

The stop was to make sure they had enough sustenance for seven days and nights. Or eight days and seven nights. Whatever. The Market, Colt noted, seemed to be "the place" to stop – at least for Bill and his climbing friends when they were heading that direction. True for a whole lot of people, apparently, as it was a hopping place. It had a big deli, even a restaurant. And there was a totem pole – a tall one … or perhaps it just seemed tall to Colton. (Many things were tall to Colton that might be just questionably tall to others.)

They had lots of stuff to consider purchasing at the Market, their final stop before heading out for the camping event. All kinds of food, drinks, and nourishment. Colton couldn't remember the items they picked up there … maybe more energy bars or packaged noodles. They did not get a lot as Bill was pretty well-prepared. They definitely didn't need any toilet paper.

After visiting the store, fueling up on sandwiches – the last possibly for several days – the guys were then on their way to the wilderness, literally – The Buckhorn Wilderness of Olympic National Forest.

This is getting real, Colt thought.

The road they traveled next was not a freeway. Oh, it was free – as in there were no tolls. But there was little pavement. It was paved only part of the way, actually very little of the way, as Col recalled. The path was a good place to build a road if there were ever intentions of doing so. Regardless, he could not remember the road number or name by the time he told his story to me, and he didn't bother to look up the name or ask Bill. I didn't try to find it on a map, either. He told me the route was about twenty miles of dirt road driving.

Colton and Bill eventually arrived at a parking lot off in the woods and mountains at the Upper Dungeness Trailhead. Colton could not recall if there were other cars there on that day. He also could not describe the lot. He couldn't remember much about their arrival except that there was a lot of sunshine.

He also noted that somewhere along that road/path, they'd left the world behind them, at least in the respect that they had left behind any kind of cell service long before the trailhead. Colton was used to "holes" in the coverage back home in Indiana. But this was a giant hole, as in they were, then, in a sense, alone. Alone with nature.

The time had come to start their trek into the woods and eventually the mountains. They were going to commune with nature. They would have no outside contact with civilization until they returned.

So far, so good.

74

Everett Kunzelman

Chapter Ten

To the Woods ...

The scene was beautiful. The air. The sun. The forest. Colton was sold. And he was still in the parking lot ...

All the nature, woods, trail (anticipation of more of the trail...) – everything was fantastic! Our city boy was giddy. Almost giddy, for sure. Well, there was the forty-pound backpack, at first a shock of sorts, which he hoped would eventually become just part of the adventure. The good news was that the pack didn't cause Colton to fall over backwards when he first put it on. He somehow managed to maintain his stature, whatever that might be and as short as that was. That said, his shortness may have helped. His center of gravity was closer to the ground. So, at least, he wouldn't have fallen very far.

Bill, the great guide he was already turning out to be, had also given Colt a hiking stick. Oh, boy! Colt had never used one on any of his past hikes, though he might have occasionally picked up a limb to serve as one out on the trails near his home. He had a "pretty" one he'd acquired in Maine – but he'd never used it. He also had an "ugly" one that he used for dog walks.

As they left the lot and made it onto the trail, the forest was mystical – that's the word that seemed most descriptive, he said. Colton had a hard time describing the woods. The light was ethereal, he told me. They were surrounded by ancient trees of generations, never cut, never harvested. That was special to him.

He did recall a wonderful wooden bridge they crossed relatively early in the trip – not exactly sure where or when that was. But it wasn't immediately. The bridge must have crossed the Dungeness River – running through the woods near the trailhead. (He figured that out later after he reviewed maps following the trip, assuming he had the correct map location to begin with.) Not sure he knew the name of the river. He probably forgot what Bill had told him.

Colt never was a good one to describe or sense smells, which somewhat limited his appreciation for the woods. Could be that he was just not paying close enough attention or not concentrating on that aspect of his experience. From our conversations, it was likely he could usually smell chocolate and, perhaps, peanut butter. Inside a house with a gas furnace and range, he was also able to pick up the slightest "leak" or smell of natural gas – the strongest smell he could pick up, he mentioned. But, as for the forest smells, he said the area there was kind of musky, kind of like mushrooms, which was different than he expected, not that he could tell me what scent he actually did expect.

Colton thought very early in the ordeal that this story could be an interesting book about their journey in the forest and mountains. Of course, he didn't think of that *before* the trip. So, he made no preparations to record any of his thoughts or sensory experiences. Then, ten years later, when he decided to try putting the details to paper and share the story, some facts were forever buried or gone, and the book he would have written would be more fictional than a historical accounting. Or so he thought. A book about a walk in the woods had already been written, though. At least, one was titled as such. Oh, he could use a different title. He was on a hike, not a walk, anyway. "A Hike in the Woods" sounded just a little too similar to the other title. It might create some confusion. Beyond that, he would have to continue to ponder if he even wanted to write a book. Ultimately, he decided to use a storyteller (me, as you know). So, despite the various holes and forgotten details, we're making an effort.

Back to the ordeal I'm attempting to capture …

That first day of hiking was to Col a lot like many of the treks back home, in a general sense. If there was an elevation change that first part of the trip, it was subtle or gradual or slight enough to avoid any serious recognition or concern. He had no need to stop and rest. He didn't feel the need to start telling stories of days gone by. All was well. Extra oxygen was not required – not that there was any in his backpack, that he knew of.

On the hiking trail that first afternoon and early evening, they were at times on a wide trail that was more open, and at other times, they were on a pretty narrow one. Same trail, just different looks. Well-worn, though, in either regard. The trail wasn't dusty, nor wet. Well-packed down might accurately describe the surface. Not much in the way of markings or signs existed. There were no mile markers, for example, which he recalled seeing in some of the Indiana state park trails. No "less than a JW" experience yet!

Colton thought the trail was well-worn because people could make the hike THAT far before turning back – like doing a day-hike from the trailhead. *Wimps.* Then he thought that might be an unfair judgement, at least until he had arrived at his first campsite and himself survived the first night.

Colt could not recall whether or not they saw people along their first afternoon route. For some reason, he thought they might have near the bridge, but he wasn't sure. There was no wildlife, either. It was a pretty quiet journey, just Bill telling him things, like the river's name, which he'd forgotten.

There was a healthy pile of, uh, poop along the trail – awfully close to the human traffic areas along the trail, he added. Bill identified that as bear scat. So, bears do, well, you know – sh** in the woods. It was a little disconcerting to Col knowing there were bears around, but it wasn't, as of yet, a major impediment to his impending adventure.

Colton was uncertain how far they hiked, but the journey seemed a fair distance for that first day, longer than most of his hikes back home. Turned out to be only a few miles. Still longer than most single trails back home in Indiana. They ended up near the river (or a creek that flowed into the river), but nonetheless, it was a true "babbling brook" in the area of Camp Handy (lots of places he learned the names of later or re-learned after forgetting what Bill had initially told him). There was so much sound from the water flowing through the slight rapids. The smells were those of a wet environment, which made sense. More so, though, he noted the emotional sense of being so refreshed. It was peaceful and pleasant.

Camp Handy, Col later learned, was about 600 feet higher than the parking lot where they had left the car. Compared to most Indiana hikes back in the day, that change in and of itself was already near, if not over, the top of his experience in elevation changes on any single hike. All the hikes back home went up and down and around and through the woods. And that's all he knew about them. He indicated that he was certain now, years later, that those Indiana hikes were not significant in any change of elevation. They just couldn't be. The highest point in the entire state of Indiana is only a little over 1,200 feet. The mean elevation is about 700 feet.

Near that babbling brook was where Col set up his very first tent. Ever. With zero experience. Packed neatly in the backpack, the tent was for one individual, two if they really liked each other a lot. Long enough for a short person. Bill had his own – and he was taller, but Colton didn't do any comparison of the tents as to size or length. There was no tape measure in the backpack ... no room for that.

He couldn't remember the color or colors of said tents, either. One or both could have been blue. Or green. Or not.

He said it was interesting how the thing "popped" into shape, and reasonably well, too, after some rudimentary assembly. He took great pride in not having destroyed it while trying to "build" the thing. He recalled the tent had a zipper "door", if you want to call the opening a door. Maybe, it's considered a window? Or an entrance? Whatever. He thought it may have had a padded layer on the bottom. The story really isn't about the tent, but it was obviously important to Colton.

Colton had a sleeping bag he had had for a couple of years or so. He wasn't sure how long. Green. He still has the sleeping bag, he says, packed away somewhere. The bag was rated to some temperature below zero, he thought, which was not required on the Olympic area trip. The last time he used the sleeping bag was when he stayed at a "vacation home" he and his wife had bought. There was construction going on to make the place livable, having been purchased as a foreclosure. He took his older dog, Indy, with him to visit one weekend. (The older dog was a Golden Doodle – and no, he wasn't referring to his wife …) He had an air mattress then, too. (Not sure he still had that, he said.) And he took a dog bed for Indy to use. Sometime during the night (it could have been rather early in the night), Indy decided the air mattress looked pretty good – better than her bed – and she crawled up on the mattress next to Dad. She did not insist on getting into his sleeping bag or making him move off of the air mattress completely. That may have been the beginning of his older dog sleeping in the bed with him for the rest of the dog's life. The start of something big as far as habits go, right? A new routine. A life in transition.

And we transition back to our main feature …

Near the spot they chose to camp was a firepit of sorts, very much like one Col thought you might see cowboys or indigenous people hanging around. Or even Tonto and the Lone Ranger on television (which he realized aged him). There were rocks in a circular pattern. But it wasn't a huge firepit. And it didn't have the appearance of ashes inside of it – just dirt. No one told stories. Or sang.

Colt seemed to hum a lot, by the way. The tune was incomprehensible, always, but there were tones coming out. Singing? Not as much, but occasionally. Likely best that singing was only sporadic for, try as he might, he was not going to find recording music as a line of work to secure as a second career. He loved music, though, and always seemed to be listening to some kind. He had quite wide-ranging tastes too.

As for the food that first night, Col could not recall in his life ever having eaten ramen noodles or whatever kind of noodles they had. There was no pizza. No steak over the fire. They had noodles. Gluten-free noodles. Whatever brand or type Bill had made them buy. And the water came from the stream through the filtering device Bill had brought along. This was all very foreign to Colton. Very austere. The thought crossed his mind that the gluten-free nature of the food might help with the IBS threat, but the water might counterbalance that, if their water filter didn't do its job. Who knew for sure? But he supposed they'd find out.

The water filtering unit, which may have been what Bill called a Sweetwater pump, was a hand-pumped device that sucked the water from the stream (or other water source) through a filter that would provide, good and clean drinking (or cooking) water for hikers/campers. Colton didn't use the device himself, preferring to leave the purification process to the veteran. He did not want to mess that up. It seemed to be a relatively important function. Watching Bill over the entire adventure use the purifier, though, it seemed reasonably easy to operate and definitely easier than hauling water in their backpacks.

For their food preparation, there was a pot and a heating device. Well, there was a burner (Bill called the piece of equipment a "pocket rocket") and then a fuel canister. It could have been one unit. Not sure. The pot sat on a frame over the heat source/burner. Col could not remember the fuel they used. Camping fuel – it had to be that, right … whatever that is – likely a Coleman product of some kind. It sure was easier than building and then lighting a fire from brush and twigs. Easier to put out, too. Easier to leave nothing behind, which was their goal as well as a requirement. Regardless, Colton took no interest in learning much about "the kitchen".

Colt was not too sure at first about actually drinking the water and eating the noodles cooked in said water. Becoming ill from the water (or anything else) was not in what might be termed "Plan A". Of course, that first night, Col didn't know how his city boy bodily system would react to filtered water from the wild. But, to his delight, he did perfectly fine! He didn't need any excess toilet paper … yet.

Bill had brought them a little refreshment, other than water post-purified. That was a great extra load to bear. And Colt appreciated his friend's sacrifice. Red wine was good for the soul and the mind and even had some health benefits – if consumed in moderation. And they were definitely inside the moderation parameters with the small amount they had. Whether cabernet or another red – or the real "rotgut" that Bill mentioned – there was no being described by color, smell, taste, body, or structure. There was no swirling in a glass. They just drank it! The forest was no place for wine snobs.

While sitting around the campfire, not telling wild stories but stories all the same, they shared a bit about their upbringing and found commonality. Neither came from anything close to exorbitant wealth, but from different kinds of financially supported and assisted families.

"I suppose," Bill offered, "there was wealth, but it was in the form of caring about each other and making life work. Not 'wealth' in the way many might define it."

"Now that is meaningful. Money cannot buy that, can it?" Col offered.

Bill agreed and added, "We did get food handouts from the government. There was peanut oil, corn meal, and other things, but I remember most how lousy the turkey thighs were. Terrible. And I still hate turkey."

Colton then noted that he, too, had eaten food from an agency. "What I recall most was the peanut butter. That was bad. The cheese was so-so. Seems to me that we had bologna, perhaps? I cannot remember. We concocted something my grandma called 'ham salad'. Never cared for ham after that … likely that was the bologna and whatever she used without ham, but it ruined ham for me. And I remember another time that a labeling ruined something … my younger daughter loved mushrooms on pizza until I asked her if she knew they were a fungus. Not sure she ever recovered…"

They had more in common than just their careers. Neither admitted to being a mass murderer, though. And there were no arrest histories. Their bonding was expanded, though, from the industry committee meetings they'd attended to get them to where they were now – camping in the Olympics.

As they prepared for the night's sleep, Colton had already set up his tent closer to the water flowing by. Bill was a little farther back from the stream, but close enough. It did not occur to Colton that Bill might know something and, hence, had chosen to set up his tent where he did. But that was not the case, as all was turning out great so far that night! The peaceful sound of the water rushing by surrounded them. All was going so well.

And then …

That peacefulness was shattered a bit as Col watched Bill hang their food on a line fifteen feet or so above the ground.

"Why are you doing that?" Colton asked.

Oh, there was a reason ...

"In the event bears show up, the food will not be within their reach," Bill said, as if it were the most normal thing to do.

That's when the reality of "camping in the wild" really sunk in for Colt.

The earlier scat was just out there – this was more personal, and much more real. Colt hadn't yet seriously considered wildlife in their camp, when they were sleeping. Except for snakes … and you know he always thought of snakes. But otherwise, he never had been concerned about wildlife … not in his backyard, but yeah, he was no longer in his backyard, was he?

Regardless, with "lights out" meaning the sun was down, there was still a sort of peacefulness that settled in around and within his tent. The creek or river or brook, whatever it was, was all Colton heard. He wasn't sure a bear would have even had to tread quietly that night – after getting up super early for his flights, two airport jaunts, the drive to the ferry, the drive to the market and then the trail, and the walk/hike (*He was HIKING!*), he was wiped out and ready for some rest. The wine may have helped a little. He had no concern about bears as sleep captured his awareness and set his mind free to dream.

Chapter Eleven

Going Up

Colt's first night camping was a success – on awakening, he realized he had actually fallen asleep, even knowing of the "wildlife" potential, and he did not recall any nightmares or even any dreams at all. Before sleep came, he remembered the sound of the water flowing down the stream. It had been a great first night in the hinterland. No JW, just great sound piped in by nature.

Colton had always loved the sound of rapids, waves, or any sound of water. He used to study for exams or continuing education, like FINRA (Financial Industry Regulatory Authority), using a CD of an ocean shoreline. The rapids that first night camping did not have crashing of waves, but it was still the sounds of water, and he enjoyed it.

His goal to actually sleep in a tent in the wild had been achieved. Life was good. Time to go home!

Well … no, it wasn't … nope … there was an adventure ahead. There were more "firsts" to come. That was just Night Number One.

Their food was untouched, still hanging high above the rocks of their campfire circle. All was well. All appendages were present.

The first breakfast after the first night's sleep in a tent in the wild was oatmeal – the breakfast of hikers. Bill's question of, "How would you like your omelet?" was, in retrospect, cruel. There was no toast either. Nor bacon. There was an air of bacon present – but only in Colton's mind. *What kind of breakfast doesn't have bacon? Golly.* But Colton loved oatmeal – he could eat it every day. There had been stretches in his breakfast preparation life, for example, where oatmeal was what he ate. Every. Single. Day. That said, he'd never had the same sort of stretch with noodles for dinner. But oatmeal, yes – although he also went months without it. Oatmeal was somewhat seasonal.

"So, you only like noodles once in a while? Does that mean only once every twenty-four hours?" Bill teased.

Col, not knowing what the dinner menu might look like, didn't want to suddenly appear uncooperative and offered, "Well, not more than once every twenty-four hours." *That might work out.*

Their walk in the woods restarted after their non-bacon breakfast was completed. And yes, it was a hike, not a walk. Not far after leaving their first campsite, they encountered the first humans of the projected seven-day outing. No more than a mile or so out, they came upon a huge father of a man and his tiny daughter crossing a small bridge in the opposite direction. (Might be that bridge Col kind of remembered earlier, but now it was being relocated to its proper place.) The girl couldn't have been much more than three or four years old, all dressed in pink. Dad was suffering under a huge load of his own gear and that of his daughter, in addition to toting a pretty impressive belly.

"Pinky" (as Bill named her) stood directly in front of him on the bridge, forcing him to stop.

"Mommy's taking a rest!" She yelled in her best "outdoor voice".

Her dad merely inquired how far was Camp Handy. The destination he and Pinky sought wasn't too much farther. Thankfully. Camp looked like an important destination for him.

The rest of the way out of that immediate area, Col and Bill were expecting to see "Mommy". Finally, though, they surmised that she must actually be taking her well-earned rest at home by sending her daughter and "Dad" out into the wild for the weekend. It made Col wonder if parents back in his early years were all excited to see their kids wander off to a state park for the day. That might have been the peace the parents longed for … just a thought.

Colt and Bill were initially on the Upper Dungeness Trail, headed to what Colton understood was Constance Pass Trail. And that was what the trail was. Bill said the pathway was named Home Lake Trail before the national park's boundary line.

Once onto the new trail, the sort of wandering footpath had more of a pitch to it than the one they'd traveled the first day, but it also had areas where they encountered flatter areas – well, they weren't exactly flat, but they weren't steep either. A mixed bag. Not all straight up, but never truly flat.

The trees of the forest were thinning out some, and it was drier than down by the river in the lower land. Now and then, there were glimpses through the trees of what was ahead. Colton could not recall if this is where they started to encounter a sign every so often. But one sign he remembered welcomed him to Olympic National Park property. Bill was also welcomed. And to Colton's delight and relief, the sign didn't say, "DON'T BE LIKE COLTON!". The welcoming sign explained there were rules in the park, not applicable in the Buckhorn Wilderness and National Forest they'd just left, such as different rules about campfires. He could not remember the exact differences but, to Colt, the sign was a big confirmation that they weren't just following wild animal paths into the brush, perhaps to their dens or dinner tables. There were apparently rules in the forest too.

Speaking of brush, later that second day included another brush with humanity. There were tents.

They were in an area among a large number of boulders. Huge boulders. This was the area known as Boulder Shelter, a great place to camp. There were smells of wildflowers and kind of an alpine smell – possibly "subalpine" caught in the breeze from higher up the mountain – and, to be clear, the path was constantly higher up. Bill told him (and reminded him later) that there were numerous flowers like columbine and Columbia tiger lilies and others. But back to the tents …

There were tents in the area, but tent dwellers were not around. Wildlife was, though, which led Colt's mind back to wondering if the tent dwellers had left their tents to follow the wild animal tracks into the woods. At that point, the thought had not been seriously considered that the tents might be abandoned due to wildlife itself coaxing the humans down the trail … as in "run for your lives" coaxing. It wasn't likely. Not at all likely, right?

This was also the time of their first encounter with anything living in the wild – excluding bugs (and there weren't many of those that he remembered, just a few). The critters were marmots.

Marmots.

Not bears. Not elk. Not cougars. Not mountain goats. Not deer. Not snakes. None of those creatures. Marmots.

Col had never seen a marmot in his life. Life had been good – and now, it was even better! The first one they saw was sitting on top of a big boulder. He didn't recall that one making any sound. (Oh, and for those of you who don't know, a marmot is a large ground squirrel type creature.)

"Are marmots gluten-free?" Colton asked. (Naturally, he would ask that, thought I, your narrator.)

"Yes, but let's let the critter live for now – we are good so far. Don't want to carry any more weight in or on the pack just yet," Bill wisely answered.

Colt figured the marmot would have to hang from the backpack. Extra weight, yes. And an attraction for bigger beasts. Not that he could catch a marmot anyway. He and his dogs couldn't even catch squirrels. Well, they did one time the year before this trek, but then, they didn't know what to do with it. The squirrel sat there looking at them with a slightly injured rear leg. The dogs stood there looking at the rodent. "What do we do now, Dad?" *City dogs.* He ended up taking the dogs in the house. The squirrel sat there about ten minutes and then hobbled up a tree, somewhat slowed, but pretty much unscathed.

Colton may have suggested to Bill that he could always claim the animal was a bigger and meaner creature when he got back home. But to allow Colton to get by with that seemed a little dishonest, so, once again, they were marmots.

There was a fair walk (or hike) through the trees and such, and then Colton recalled that they started to seriously go up, following narrow paths between boulders, around trees, and even switchbacks. ("Switchbacks", in hiking, are sections of a trail where a steep mountain or hill is approached, up or down, by a trail that makes sharp turns back and forth to reduce the steepness. "Hairpin turns" might be what you would call a road that has "switchbacks".) There was a general direction to go, and Bill seemed to know it, and that was up. The effort required challenged the city boy some and made his hikes back home seem somewhat simplistic. Okay … very simplistic. The journey was becoming much rougher, enough so to cause him, at times, to pause and gaze across the mountains. He needed to catch his breath. Rest his legs. So, yeah, it wasn't just a gaze … the kind where you stop to smell the flowers, which were plentiful, at least.

Colt tried his best to keep up between rest breaks. He did fall behind Bill a few times – I mean, his legs are and were much shorter than Bill's. That was his explanation. Or excuse. And, no, he said his feet did not hurt. His boots were still wonderful! So far, so good, he thought. When he did fall behind Bill, he was never really sure how far behind he actually was. He just knew that, a few times, he couldn't see Bill up the mountain ahead of him. But he never did get lost. The trail was worn sufficiently for one to know where to go. And he would always catch up – probably because Bill waited for him, although he never found Bill having the need to take a nap while waiting.

Still going up, suddenly, they reached a flat area on top of a ridge that was fairly open. There were higher mountains around, but they enjoyed a wide, expansive view. This was on what was known as Del Monte Ridge, not too far beyond Constance Pass. The area seemed a perfect setting for a campsite. The ridge did go on for some distance, offering options.

"Del Monte Ridge," Bill said, "named after a cook for the Boy Scouts in the 1920's. Great views."

And there were great views.

Colton and Bill set up camp near a drop off, which was modest in degree of descent versus a sheer cliff. Still, if you rolled down it, you might roll a spell – a long spell – and pick up a good deal of speed. Sleepwalkers should probably be discouraged from setting up camp there unless they were able to competently maintain footing while asleep.

Rock formations were also near them on the ridge; a rock shelter for climbers is how Bill described it. Now, they were climbers, too? Yes, Bill was, but Col was barely a hiker.

The additional part of the story was that, at times, the winds on that ridge would howl and blow with great intensity. Climbers (and hikers) would set up in the rock shelter to avoid being blown off the mountain, down the slope, all the way to the boulders. Luckily, there was no wind that day. Bill said that was unusual and only happened a few days a year.

Colton, thinking his low-profile height worked in his favor (for clarification, yes, in a horizontal position, pretty much all are near equal in height), set up camp outside the rock shelter nearer the small drop off to the east or northeast, taking his chances on sleepwalking or any wind that might whip up overnight. Bill, however, set up camp in the shelter. He deserved that shelter, Colton decided, because he was a "climber". And since Col was not a sleepwalker, though he may be a talker in his sleep once in a while, he rolled the dice and hoped nothing changed during the night.

The setting that night was as spectacular as the stream, but in several different ways ...

The ridge was quiet. No sound of water charging over rocks.

The air seemed dry, despite snow on the mountains around them at higher elevations. There was, as noted, almost no wind.

They could see the lights of a town miles away down the mountain through a pass or a valley of some kind to the east. Colton was not sure what town or city it was. They were very small lights from their vantage point, though. Likely the town was on or near Puget Sound. (Looking up the possibilities on a map later made him think the town was most likely Triton. That hamlet was at the right trajectory across the landscape and sat on or near a small peninsula.) Regardless, that night, it was hard to see any detail from that far away. They had no binoculars (no room in the backpack and too much weight).

They watched the sun set as the moon was rising on the opposite side. *Perfect timing!* That was simply spectacular!

Bill mentioned years later, when he and Colt were reminiscing about the journey, that to the best of his recollection, that spot was the best campsite he had ever experienced. The only negative – which did not count for much – was the distance to water. There just wasn't anything real close on the ridge near them. Bill reminded Colton that they had to go down the mountain to a snowfield to find water, recalling that the trip was quite a hike, but worth every step to be able to camp where they did.

Dinner that night was noodles. Another personal record scored with two dinners in a row of noodles. They were fine. He did not think to ask Bill if there was something else to be consumed for the next day. Surely it wouldn't be more noodles. Not three days in a row. No!

Again, they did not see any wildlife – even anymore marmots. Colton could not recall what they did with the food that second night because there were not a lot of trees up there.

Or were there any trees at all? Yes, he thought there were some, but they were about 6,000 feet up, so trees were sparse and, the ones there were, they were shorter. Bill mentioned that he had seen mountain goats on that ridge in previous visits at that very spot where they camped. But not that night. They had no visitors.

There were a few times the sound of rocks falling could be heard, and they appeared to be falling from Mount Constance, which was sort of east of them. It was no earthquake, just large, falling rocks.

The distance covered on that first full day was a fair piece, as they say in some places back home in Indiana. The net elevation change that day, which from the camp to the ridge was roughly 3,000 feet up, might have totaled most all of the changes on every single one of Colton's Indiana hikes put together and then multiplied by a decent size number. That elevation change, in a single day, was a major one for Colt, a personal record, for sure.

His memory of the babbling brook seemed like a long, long time ago on a trail far, far away versus just that morning. And there was a sense of tiredness – the forty-pound pack, the elevation, the distance, all of that added up as Colton appreciated the time to relax a bit. His legs, back, arms, every part he had, was experiencing a little achiness. But that could have been true for even an experienced hiker, he reasoned.

Col mentioned he had a small note pad and a pen. He took notes of some events of the day, intending to do so every day. (He couldn't recall what happened to that notebook. Might have helped some, now that he was trying to recall the specifics, but who wants the embellished tale to be crushed with actual facts?)

Still, he seemed to recall jotting down highlights once in a while, and he specifically remembered doing so that second night.

Falling asleep was far easier for him that night. And he noted his feet didn't hurt that much. Although everything else hurt. And he was tired. The moon above, which was nearly full, could not keep his attention and defer sleep.

And sleep did indeed come …

Everett Kunzelman

98

Chapter Twelve

Late July/Early August/Summer Snow Fall

Morning came and Colton's tent was where it had been placed the night before – no gusts of wind had carried him away. Could be considered a good gamble, luck, or nature having given him a pass for being adventuresome.

The new day was sunny. Thankfully, Bill and Colt had not experienced any rainy days or nights thus far – actually, there were not many clouds. A beautiful day in the neighborhood of the forests and mountains. The real camping experience really needed a rainy night, perchance, but it wasn't an absolute requirement. Later in the journey perhaps? Not that it was hoped for.

Breakfast was uneventful. Still no omelet. Or bacon. Just oatmeal. Loving oatmeal meant that the new camper – that would be Colt – was not complaining about breakfast. Besides, he had never learned to make omelets like you see real cooks do. They toss them in the air and all that fancy action. Or was that for making pizza? Mixing stuff into a scrambled egg creation was as close as he could get to an "omelet". Someday, maybe, he would try to perfect his omelet prowess for an egg breakfast or meal.

Even under some pressure, from me, Colt could not recall having coffee on the outing in the Olympics. Knowing that he could live without coffee may have been an unintended consequence of achieving his hiking goal, who knows? Many of us don't have a coffee requirement, despite being coffee drinkers – Col and I agreed on that.

"Growing up at my grandma's house, I never remember having coffee in the house," he said.

"You grew up at your grandma's house?" Bill asked.

"Yep. She raised three of us."

"Another similarity, in part," Bill noted. "I grew up in my grandma's house, but Mom raised us."

"My mom was around at times," Colt added, "but Grandma was the constant. My dad had left by the time I was about age two or three."

"Eerie or strange … my dad died when I was about five. Don't remember much of those early years. Memories from early childhood for both of us might be painted in another's eyes."

"Sorry about your dad. Where did that analogy come from – 'painted in another's eyes'? Pretty good one," Colton responded.

"That was a "Bill Original". No charge."

Not exactly the same experiences, but there were several parallels. Both of them had experienced very similar childhoods.

But then the hike down the trail continued ...

They were headed for Sunnybrook Meadows, a little off the beaten path, off the primary trail that is, but close. The trail was still Constance Pass Trail, headed down toward the Dosewallips River. The meadow was higher up the mountain side, not that far from the long ridge, before the trail took a very nice downward plunge, with twists and turns as the elevation took a big dive.

The Pacific Northwest Trail had been created about a year prior to their escapade as a general name applied to several trails that all connect, including Constance Pass Trail. If you followed the new general trail west, you would end up at the coast of the Pacific Ocean. If you went the other direction, kind of easterly, you would end up in Glacier National Park in Montana (eventually), at which point you should be able to then connect to another trail that would connect you with still other trails, all the way to the Atlantic coast including, for a time, the Appalachian Trail in New Hampshire, where Colton and his daughter had done the terrible interview of the experienced hiker years prior. There could be a gap or two – Colton wasn't sure –

but, for the most part, the trail could be considered to be coast to coast. The "locals" and those familiar with the Olympic area trails still go by the earlier trail names, even years after the new trail's creation or, rather, its recognition or naming, or whatever it's called.

Regardless, getting lost while just off the trail, heading toward the nearby meadow, seemed incredibly difficult to make happen. Well, I suppose we'll see about that, won't we?

The boys – actually one of them was a 59-year-old, Colton, and Bill was roughly ten years younger – so not really "boys" at all, started across several large areas of snow, making their way across some north-facing "snowfields" as Col called them – which might be the proper name for them. The calendar was nearing the first of August, or at least mid-to-late July, so seeing snow was really quite exciting, in a weird sort of way. Bill was really surprised by how much snow there was. Not fourteen feet, but there was a lot and much more than he expected when considering the route. Some was expected – just not that much, he explained. There was definitely too much for the calendar to soon flip over to August. There was a little appreciation for said snow – a natural "air conditioner" of sorts.

Colton was slow, but he effectively navigated the fields. Well, effectively enough. Can we define "effectively" as "good enough"? Getting a little, oh, braggadocious using "effectively" could almost appear cocky. He was doing an acceptable job. How about that?

The trail at times, when they were not hiking over snow, was very narrow across the mountain side with a steep grade up the hill to the ridge and, more dramatically, down to very large boulders, those being the encouragement to avoid falling and rolling. The drop was high enough that the big rocks didn't look all that large, but they were indeed huge. If the guys fell, there very well could have been increased speed rolling. The trail location was high enough on the hillside (or mountainside) that the speed of an unfortunate fall really would be a factor by the time the boulders were reached. (That rolling speed issue was what left the greatest impression on Colton for absolutely the entire hike … that, and the fear of such a narrow little trail across a desolate mountain.) But then they would be back in snow, off the narrow mountainside path, not sure where the exact trail was.

Colt thought the sensation odd, but the narrow, open trail, just inches wide, seemed more threatening to him than the hidden, snow-covered portion. He could not help but glance down the mountain every once in a while. Could have been every step taken. He described the experience as almost like walking on a beam. Likely a psychological trick. There was likely a subconscious thought that digging into snow might be easier to slow you down than in dirt and rock? Might be true. Might not. But he really did not want to test the theory.

Once, Colton described, they ventured across a snowfield, mixed with sizeable chunks of rocks and some crevices, and then Bill realized they were not on the trail any longer, having lost their pathway in the snow. They were nearing an area with no obvious parting of the trees or any signs – which were few and far between, as they say, anyway – and it was more downhill than Bill remembered. So, they backtracked a bit, wandering around, which was good for Colton's practicing of walking on the ice and snow. Finally, they found what they thought was the trail. Having been on the trail previously helped Bill eventually gain the proper perspective. And everything was back in order.

The once snow-hidden path became more apparent and somewhat out of the snow.

Colton thought later – years later – that Bill knew where they were the whole time, every single minute, but recognized the need for Colton to practice walking on the snow and so created the "unfamiliar moment" versus just asking him to practice. *Very good ploy.*

They made their way through a bunch of these snow (and sometimes icy) fields. Very slow for Colton, despite the practice while "trail hunting". Bill, on the other hand (or foot), walked as if he was taking a stroll in town. Experience. Impressive. At the time, though, Col spent much more of his time watching his own footing than being impressed with Bill's graceful saunter.

After five or six or so of the snowfields, there came another one, and it was a little different.

This one was more south-facing, more likely southwest. The directional change was somewhat evident as the sun was making the mountainside glisten more than on the previous fields. "Down" was then left in the new area, whereas it was right in the previous snowfields. They must have crossed the ridge. Trees were closer together down the mountain on the new side than the boulders on the north-facing ones, but still down a bit and a little sparse closest to the trail, becoming much more dense way down the mountain.

Colt was making his way carefully and chatting with Bill, who was ahead of him some, probably fifteen or twenty feet, maybe more, could be less. He remembered planting his right foot in the snow and then crossing over with his left, just about to plant the left when his right foot gave way. He was on his way downhill. There were no guardrails. No safety belt. No path in sight. And no sled.

Somehow, Col held onto his hiking pole, holding the staff up in the air as he slid down the mountain on his backpack. There was no digging into the snow to slow him down. He was going way too fast for that. He hit the first tree, a smaller one, somewhat shorter anyway, and spun around, briefly heading down the mountain backwards. He then hit tree number two, which was about the same size as tree number one, from his perspective, though that was somewhat warped by his increasing speed and lack of any control over his descent. Both trees were some sort of cedar or in that class of those with needles. The second one flipped him around forward, and he found himself almost immediately airborne over some fallen trees and then bouncing on others when – SMACK! – he slammed into a bigger cedar tree, face first with his arms around the thing, still somehow holding his pole.

All he could hear was Bill yelling, "Don't move! Don't move! Don't move!" … over and over and over.

Colt wasn't sure how many times he said that, but, golly, he wasn't really in the frame of mind at that moment to move much anyway. So, he sat there, his forehead against the tree, hugging the thing (or at least he kept his arms around it).

A real, down the mountainside, tree hugger he was.

When Bill arrived, he explained his fear that Colt might have been impaled by a dead branch or two. Or broken a leg or arm or rib. Or had a closed head injury – and yes, there were times that might have been suspected without the fall. But, no, he was not impaled, though there were two dead branches at his lower chest level, one to his right and one to his left, perfectly placed with his projectile of a body between them. And there were no broken bones or serious damage otherwise.

He was alive!

Chapter Thirteen

Seeking Flat Land

There Colton sat, hugging the tree … and still holding his hiking pole. The thought of being impaled hadn't sunk in completely, but completely enough that his forehead went back against the tree for support.

Bill did a much better job than Colton would have ever done in asking all the right questions about his condition. Where did he have pain – any pain or great pain – was there any injury that needed a tourniquet, how many fingers was he holding up. If the situation had been reversed, Col's inquiry would have been limited to, "Are you okay?"

There were a lot of scratches and a fair amount of blood.

One weird thought Colt recalled having was, "I wonder how far a bear can smell blood?"

Anyway, nothing was broken. Nothing was bleeding profusely and therefore required a tourniquet. There were no severe bumps that were overly painful. Oh, there were some that were mildly painful, possibly, that were perchance overshadowed by his overall realization that he was pretty much in good shape, considering. He might have been too excited that he'd survived to feel all the painful locations, too excited there were trees to stop him before he made it all the way down the mountain to the river. Nothing appeared to be twisted or sprained too badly. His head appeared to be fine – as fine as any head could be after a little roll and spin down a mountainside. (Could be as fine as Colton's head would ever be anyway ... just a thought.)

They relaxed a little while Col used the plentiful snow to clean off a lot of the blood, still wondering about the capability of a bear's proficiency for smell. One deep gouge was going to leave a mark (and did, on his left thigh), but nothing came really close to requiring stitches. There were a lot of bumps and scrapes, the obvious result of an uncontrolled descent through snow and trees down a mountain.

"I have a friend who fell down a mountain with a backpack. She was in Utah. I think Anne said they were at the Uinta Mountains somewhere. That could have been Utah," Colt mumbled.

"Yes, that's in Utah," Bill answered, interpreting Colt's mumbling the best he could. "It's the only mountain range that runs east and west in the United States, as I recall. Might have learned that in mountain class. As for riding the backpack down or 'turtling' a friend of mine was killed thirty years ago in the Cascades taking that kind of route, so that is dangerous. You could have been seriously hurt today. Really."

"Yep. Lucky I am. Anne said her slide was full of boulders. She wasn't hurt but took a ride on the pack down a bit of the mountain. Can't remember which one exactly. Not sure if there was snow or ice. Now we can share stories," Colt added.

And then he finally blurted out the question he was dying to know the answer to, "How far can a bear smell blood?"

"Oh, fifty miles …," Bill said and then paused.

Colt could feel anguish fan out across his face.

Bill laughed and then continued, "Well, several miles anyway, upwind, but I've read they might be able to smell up to twenty miles. That wouldn't necessarily be a scratch that they could smell that far. Maybe a dead body."

"It's a good thing I didn't catch that marmot, hauling that carcass with me down the mountain."

"Good point," Bill agreed.

"Wow! Look at that gash!" Col, the mountain slider, commented.

The reality was that there wasn't THAT much blood. Oh, a little. But not like there was a dead carcass now on the side of the mountain. There was no pool of blood. But apparently, bears can smell as well as or better than most any animal on Earth. And yet, Colton was wandering into knowledge territory he really didn't want to explore right then.

Let it go, he coached himself.

Bill figured they were about twelve to fifteen or so miles from the car – a decent trek. Not as far as Colton thought, but he really had no good idea or any kind of frame of reference for where they were. Initially, Bill thought they were nearly twice that far. Bill also figured they were about the same distance in miles from the nearest ranger station, which was more or less in the opposite direction or, at least, a different direction than the one in which they were headed. He was not as sure about that location, though, as he'd never needed one before. Thankfully, there was really no need for one at this time, either. No 911 call was required. Not that they had cell service to make the call anyway.

Then Colton wandered into a subject matter he could and should have left alone ...

"What if we needed help?" he asked.

"Well," Bill responded slowly, "I might have left you here, and I would have taken off for the ranger station. They might then be able to bring a helicopter out, not that they have one at the station. Probably plenty of daylight left to get one out here from somewhere, though."

"And I would stay here and fight off any bears with my pole?"

"Sure," Bill answered. "Or snakes ..."

Such exciting opportunities, opportunities Colt neither required or desired. He was able to abandon his anxiousness, to set his concerns aside, choosing not to worry about non-issues. After all, it wasn't yet the middle of the night when some of these kinds of questions would invariably not allow him to sleep.

"I was in a helicopter once. Might have been the mid '70's in Missouri. Glass-bottomed touristy one," offered Colt. "Must have been down in the Ozarks, among all those lakes, near that music town."

"Branson?"

"Yes. That's it, Branson," Colton concurred. "Glad I don't need a medical emergency ride on one."

"Yep. They couldn't land here, you know … they would have to lower a basket to pick you up. Or just lower a rope, and you would try to hang on. That would be exciting, wouldn't it? The reality is that these rescues happen. Had two friends hauled out by helicopter from a nearby range. One had a broken leg. Then there was a friend hiking in the Cascades who tore his patella tendon. Scary stuff. Accidents happen, even with experienced people – and you're a rookie."

"Way too exciting for a rookie to be airlifted out," lamented Colton, who generally was also fearful of heights.

Despite the lack of any broken bones or ravenous wounds, Colt's body felt like there had, indeed, been an event including falling (or sliding) down a mountain, hitting trees and logs, and flying into things. One knee – as he recalled, it was his left one – had some joint pain, but just enough to slow him down versus require building a sled to pull him. Speaking of which, he did not recall discussing the sled option. His knee hurt a tad more with use, versus just sitting there. But he hoped the pain would wear off.

Try as he might, Col could not smell blood … a great thing!

Bill decided that the best decision might be to take an "easier" way back than he had planned. Now, perhaps he was then thinking about the eventual need of the sled option, but neither of them talked about that out loud. He admitted that his intention had been to traverse the mountains following a different route back to the car, although the exact conditions where he wanted to go weren't clear. (Colton later learned that Bill had originally planned a trip to Deception Basin and then over to Royal Basin from there, along with some side passages. The snow had surprised him a little already. What other unknowns lurked in the trees and mountains and passes and basins were, naturally, unknown. Unknown unknowns. Versus known knowns or unknown knowns. Whatever.) Bill decided they might essentially end up going back the way they came, with a few slight changes, likely checking out some of the side trails, depending on how Colton responded to more hiking while using his now lame knee.

Well, the reverse trail was backwards – that's a change right there. There was also the possibility of cutting the hiking and camping adventure short by a few days. For now, they headed back toward Home Lake, where they could camp for the night and then decide, after some sleep, on the next leg of the ordeal.

Bill did not point out the bear scat they passed as they approached the target area at a different angle from where they had first arrived. That didn't come up until later, during their reminiscing phase.

"Anne told me another story about hiking that I thought was cool," Col remarked. "Anne was in Glacier National Park. She wanted a picture of a moose – they had not seen one. She noticed this deer ahead of her, flipping its tail. She was walking in the deer's direction. The deer went down a side trail and looked back, as if trying to get Anne to follow – at least, that's what Anne felt. So, she did. The deer made another turn and waited for Anne before proceeding again. Anne followed. And then a little farther and through the trees, they came to a clearing, and there was a moose at a lake or pond drinking. She seems to think the deer led her to the moose. Nice positive story."

"And we have not yet seen deer or elk," Bill offered. "There are no moose here, but there are Roosevelt Elk."

I doubt a deer would lead you down a path to a bear's dinner table, Colton thought. But then, they ate his hostas back home, so they might not be the innocent creatures they appeared to be.

Getting to the lake and some rest in the shortest time required moving across an ice field. Ice. There was no snow about it. And it was very slippery. Essentially a glacier (to Colton). Slipping there led you straight down the mountainside and into the lake. The ice, in fact, formed a perfect slide right into Home Lake. *Joy.* Looked almost as if it were constructed by nature for that exact purpose.

Col never thought he'd need a life jacket on this adventure. You see, he still didn't know how to swim. At age 59 and three-quarters. So, he took some basic, extremely careful steps at the edge and then looked across the sheet of ice. *Wow!*

Anyway, no fear was to be had. Bill was able to anchor a line into the ice and fundamentally swing Colt across the ice field and then behind or among some trees to the other side. At that point, Col could make his way down through the trees, which were relatively open, climbing through snow, ice, and boulders – the usual mountain stuff. *Exciting!* Small steps versus long sliding maneuvers seemed best and being as he had tried both approaches to descents, he was qualified to choose one technique over the other.

Questions popped into Colt's head as he started to make his way down toward the lake through the trees and all:

♦ How did Bill walk on the ice? (Colton would classify that in the "miracle" category, but he didn't witness his friend walk across the ice sheet.)

♦ How did he anchor the line? (Another unexplained happening, potentially another miracle.)

♦ And then, how did he swing his short, but sufficiently nourished partner in crime across the ice?

No one knew the answers to his questions. Bill was simply good at mountain stuff.

As for Colton, he was still alive and seeking a much flatter surface.

Chapter Fourteen

More, Larger Wildlife

Despite having lots of things to grab onto, Colton was quite gingerly venturing down through the mountainous terrain adjacent to the sheet of ice (or glacier, as he called it). He had no real fear of sliding into the lake as there were plenty of trees, and also rocks, to slow him down if need be. Still, it was more of a cautious journey to avoid a pinball-style bouncing down the terrain if a poorly controlled descent should once again come upon him. Aside from a slip now and then, accompanied by a frantic grab of a limb or whatever was handy, his trudge was successful.

Finally, Colton was once more on a relatively flat surface. Bill was already there and might have been there for quite a while. Another miracle. Col wasn't sure how long, but he couldn't have been there more than an hour, he thought.

The setting by the lake was very calm and very pleasant. Peaceful with the forest all around. The lake did not have the threatening look as the water did from above it on the ice sheet. The water was calm. There were no ducks or other wildlife. Col saw no fish. He did see knotted limbs along the shoreline, and even small trees that were downed and sitting in the water and on the shore.

The non-threatening look of the water did not mean Colt would suddenly take a dip. No, not at all. He wasn't even going to try wading. Colton could not find any details later on regarding the depth of the lake; but, he did learn the distance up to Constance Pass was almost 500 vertical feet from near where they were, although the "glacier" may not have been quite that high above the water. Based on the distance he learned about Constance Pass, he guessed it was maybe close to 400 feet more down to the lake. That is a Colton-esque calculation, keep in mind, so the distance might actually be somewhat different.

Settling down after the descent reminded Colton that he was, well, not wanting to be graphic or anything, constipated or nearing that condition after two days of avoiding doing the "bear thing" in the woods, like perhaps over a fallen tree (without verification that bears use that technique). Glancing around their new campsite, on a feeble-looking wooden platform in the trees a hundred yards or so from the lake, was a commode. It was completely out in the open among the trees. *How quaint.* Let's leave that part of his story right there ... well, almost ...

Colton described to Bill the base on which the commode sat as a pretty flimsy piece of plywood. It was well-weathered, shall we say. That led to a posture in which he could consider the possibility of jumping (or hopping) if the thing collapsed. Suddenly, a felled log didn't look all that terrible. The wooden plank held, though, and the absent change of clothes was not required.

Colton set up his tent just inside the trees near the lake. There were clear and flat enough areas there to support it. Bill chose a spot just outside the trees in more of a clearing near the base of which Colton had made his way through the passage next to the glacier.

Bill used the water purifier there at the lake. Col remembered this specific use more vividly with Bill pumping the thing at the lake. He was at the edge of the water working around the downed trees and large limbs. There was a bit of a trust factor for Colton with the water, and no issues developed.

Years later, in another leap forward, if for just a moment, Bill mentioned his trust in those devices had transformed into a bit of a faith scenario, as they were no longer using the pump, but what he called a sterile pen-shaped tool they affectionately referred to as a "Jesus Stick" because the device ran on faith. "...hard to believe some UV light can effectively render your water safe, but it does," he had added. Science – a wonderful thing, in this case. For Colt, though, it had been difficult enough for him to have faith in the mechanical pump and filter used on their trip, so he figured he might pass on the UV light.

Dinner was the usual – noodles, Col's light weight delight. Three straight days. *Golly.* But no gluten meant limited time on plywood in the middle of nowhere. So, no dessert either. No chocolate cheesecake (that was Colt's personal favorite and still is) or New York style cheesecake (Bill's choice and remains so).

"I rarely order dessert in a restaurant," Colton acknowledged.

"Me, neither."

"And I do love cheesecake," Colton added, "especially chocolate cheesecake, not chocolate on the cheesecake, but chocolate through and through. There is a restaurant that seems to specialize in cheesecake that has more than one chocolate kind, as I recall, but their meal portions are so large, I rarely get dessert unless it's to go."

"So, you never learned to swim?" Bill inquired, changing the subject (possibly to avoid drooling).

"No. There was a wading pool in the Indianapolis City Park about a block or two from where I grew up. It was no swimming pool – too shallow," Colt replied. "Never remember going there, though. There was a church camp I attended way back then that did have a swimming pool. But there were no instructors that I recall. So, non-swimmers stayed on the shallow end to one side of the rope in the middle. They must have had a lifeguard or, at least, a real swimmer or two to watch over the thing. I do not remember."

"Too bad there wasn't a chance to learn."

"Yep. I guess," Colton agreed. "Not sure I can turn off the fear factor now, since I'm getting up there in years."

"I've heard that learning is harder for adults at any age," Bill replied.

He was likely correct. And that was not the time to toss Col into Home Lake to prove it.

"When we venture out here for days," Bill added, "we usually end up in a stream – kind of like a sponge bath, so to speak, or a good rinse – or take to the lake, any lake."

And then Col asked about the ice, something on his mind a lot now. "I presume that really isn't a glacier, right?"

"Depends on its persistence as an ice sheet, perhaps. Permanent ice would be. I think this is more seasonal, but it's getting late in the season. I know the ice has not been here every time I have come through here, so that chunk of ice is definitely not a glacier. Might carry over this year, though."

"Are there real glaciers around here?" Colton, the Adventurer, asked.

"There are several named glaciers … like Blue Glacier on Mount Olympus is one. That's the largest or best known, and there are others that might not have names other than the mountain they are a part of. There may be between 150 and 200 in the area in and around the park. Mount Olympus is the third-most glaciated peak in the continental United States, and it's only about eight thousand feet high … that's because of all the precipitation, like, what, two hundred feet a year."

"Well," Col said, "I don't feel too bad thinking of this sheet of ice as a glacier, then."

"Agree. A reasonable assumption."

There were a bunch of stumps at that campsite by Home Lake. "Chairs" in a rustic sense of the word. They were without arms and had no backs – like bleachers versus chairs. "Individual bleachers" would be a good descriptive name for them. Regardless of what they were called, they offered a place to sit for a moment. Not too long, but they provided a break from the upright position or from having to sit on the ground ... or on a rock. Large rocks and boulders were everywhere, none with a reclining mechanism.

"We were talking this morning about growing up. What's your earliest memory?" Colton asked.

"Let me see ..."

Bill thought about it for a bit.

"Well, *the first thing I remember was I was lying in my bed – I couldn't have been no more than one or two*," Col offered up.

And he was interrupted by Bill, who noted, "Paul, listen ..."

"Call me Al ..."

"Well, it's getting *late in the evening*," Bill continued.

Yes, time was waning in the day. At least Col didn't sing (more on that later...). But with his lyrical distraction, he couldn't recall Bill's answer to his original question about his first memory, if there even was an answer.

The decision came to call it another day. The sky was turning pale. Night was approaching. It was time to try the horizontal position. A rolling sleep came. Colt did not recall any dreams. The day had been a great one for rolling. His knee still hurt some, but not too terribly bad and not enough to keep him awake.

About 3:00 a.m. or some hour in the night (he had no watch and no phone powered up to tell him), Colton was awakened by what he thought were loud snorting noises and the sound of something relatively large walking through the brush and trees near his tent. At least the snorting sounded like it was from a larger animal. He did not believe the beast to be Bill sleepwalking.

Col remained still. No flashlight was on. The sound stopped. Was he holding his breath? Yes, some. There wasn't any food in his tent. Well, HE was in his tent and, depending on the wildlife nearby, Colton thought he could be in a select food group for the animal. He was slightly hobbled, so easy to be taken, and unable to effortlessly get away. The blood was likely dry – but it wasn't the time to check and accidentally open a wound. Besides becoming more attractive to certain beasts, he would probably exclaim "OUCH!", causing even more attention to his presence. The noisemaker slowly (it seemed like it took hours) made his or her way out of their camp and, eventually, Colton fell back to sleep.

The next morning, Colt asked Bill if he had heard the creature and, yes, he had. He said the critter sounded typical of an elk, possibly active at night due to a mountain lion encounter. Less likely, he explained that it could have also been a really loud mountain goat, based on his previous experiences out in the hinterlands. Bigger than a marmot, for sure. And a potential beast – a wild, untamed, non-domesticated animal. Most definitely.

"Well, looks like your friend's story about the deer and the moose helped us," Bill surmised. "No picture, though. The picture frame might have been filled by the elk close up just before stepping on you after blinding the animal with the flash."

"I suppose the elk weighed less being gluten-free," Colton chortled, before realizing that sometimes, one just needs to avoid trying to be funny.

Chapter Fifteen

The Meadow

While the adventure of the prior day's tumble was fresh on the hikers' minds, there was still a desire to extend the journey and not give in to a fall. They were still ready to keep wandering, making their way out to where they had not been before. They wanted to explore. To live a little. Colton especially, bad knee and all, was not ready to give in.

"Why didn't you say that yesterday?" Bill asked Colton.

"I was stumped by your question last evening."

"Now, we're all the way down here!" Bill exclaimed.

"Must be the head injury from the fall." That was the best Col could do at that moment – and yes, it was more likely a congenital, long-term condition versus a result of said fall.

Coming down, of course, meant that now, they had to go back up. Even if they went an easier way, they still must go back up. It was only five hundred feet, vertical … who wouldn't want to do that again?

So, they headed back out for Night Number Four. Somewhere out there, beneath the bright moonlight, the meadow, their desired destination, was calling to them.

Despite badgering Colton on his new sense of adventure, Bill was excited at the prospect of continuing their hike over new ground versus simply meandering back the way they'd come from. The hike would still be new, just "less new" than a totally new direction. Once their oatmeal was finished and everything was loaded, they were off again, back uphill.

They took off toward the Constance Pass Trail again, which has the Dosewallips River trail terminus or beginning – not sure which. Or both. Depends on your perspective. On this commonly traveled byway for hikers, they had not seen anyone, so far. Yes – "Pinky" and her father were on the bridge they'd gone over, but that seemed like a long time ago by now. The tents they saw earlier were off the trail just a little (most everything seemed "off the trail" to Col). Colton presumed that the tent owners had made their way back "home", after whatever had caused them to previously abandon their tents.

The trail took off from near Home Lake up toward Constance Pass – a return visit was now anticipated to the Pass and then

Del Monte Ridge. If not for the fact that Bill had more planned that he thought he actually needed to, this retreat and then change of plan might have been less welcomed. Their intermediate goal was Sunnybrook Meadows. They were a day late. And that may not be where they end up. The ultimate goal for the day was still undecided.

"Keep walking, although there is nowhere to get to really …," Bill said.

"Sounds quite poetic," Colton replied. "It's a new side of you, aside from the analogy you used yesterday."

"Well, I suppose there is poetry there, but they're not my original words – I'm quoting Rumi. And there's plenty more where that came from."

"Not much of a poet reader myself. Some," Colton responded. "But then, I love music and good lyrics, so I might be a huge poet reader, although, I suppose I would need a musical score to get into poetry. Not that I can sing."

"My climbing friends, as well as I, seem to have gotten into Rumi and similar prose. A nice respite from the banal chatter that sometimes numbs the soul."

"Sounds reasonable," Colton said. "Wish I could sing better … could be soul-numbing to listen to, at least for very long. Actually, maybe not that long. Mere minutes perhaps."

The worn trail, the actual trail, was to the side a bit of the sheet of ice Colton had swung across the day prior, with alternative paths right on up the hill. At least Bill would not have to drag the old man up the ice. They headed up through the brush, the trees, the boulders, the snow, from whence they had come the afternoon before, and they finally connected with the actual trail. It was more exciting off trail than merely wandering over to connect with the actual trail, they decided. The trail was more or less the steep path they'd been on for a couple of days – or part of it was, anyway. Or was that just a single day that they'd been on that path? Colton had lost track.

His left knee was sore. And that slowed him initially, but then he was able to kind of "walk off the discomfort" – no, he "hiked that pain away", or at least he talked himself out of being concerned about his knee at all. He did not want to be seen as ailing.

The initial climb to Constance Pass was a bit of a challenge, but, once the terrain became flatter, he began to work through his knee issue. He actually passed Bill at least once on a relatively flat area, probably because he could no longer control his gait. He had gotten that stagger-then-step move going way too fast. An altered movie line came to his mind: "[Hike] this way…"

Bill eventually reestablished the leadership role, which was a welcomed result for the boy who knew only that he was in Washington ... somewhere.

All this role sharing was happening as another beautiful day in that same neighborhood out in the wild of Washington was evolving and on full display. There was sun, and a relatively clear sky. The smell of cedar or some sort of subalpine plant life, albeit faint, wafted over the trail. The air temperature was good, despite the ice and snow all around. There were no snowball fights or snowmen – or snowwomen – built, or any snow angels made. Life was good without all of that.

Hiking by the rocks where true climbers could set up a tent seemed to remind Colton of the prior exciting day, and he inquired, "Are we headed back to the snowfields? And across that ugly one that nailed me?"

"Yes, we are," Bill confirmed.

Oh boy. The tight-rope hiking across the side of the mountain was also out there, somewhere, as well to do over again – the much more frightening feature until his grand descent.

But … the second time across the snowfields and the narrow mountain trail, and the tight rope, were uneventful. No falls. No significant slips.

They did also eliminate some of their search for the trail, assuming there was really a search the first time they went through the day prior. At least they were closer to the trail the second time around. And their tracks were the only ones in the snow (that they saw). There were no big critter footprints. Bear prints would be pretty good size, and there were none to be seen … not that Col would have recognized them as such, anyway. Bill might have, though. I suppose he could have just not told Col (a good move, if true). Whatever the truth was, it remained that there were no tracks which looked extremely large. Bill told Colt that he and his friends saw bear almost every hike out there. That wasn't exactly the welcoming words Col desired to hear, but the truth shall set you – what? – set you up for success?

This second time around, Colton gained some insight into navigating the snow without all the drama. He thought they should just traverse lower on the mountain, reducing the journey down, but then, Bill pointed out that Colton had stopped his wild descent quite far from the very bottom, so more opportunity was there to make an even longer freefall slide, quite possibly all the way to the river, bouncing from tree to tree and boulder to boulder, missing the tree that had stopped him the day before.

Opportunities are grand, aren't they?

"Let's go over the walking-on-snow suggestions again," Colt requested.

And they did. Without a whiteboard. With just a discussion, Bill waving his arms to amplify the finer points.

Although a little slower than might have been expected given the "practice" and the discussion, the two did succeed in crossing the south (or southwest) facing snowfield. Being earlier in the day might have accounted for less sun doing too much softening of the snow. Or maybe it was that Colton was just lucky the second time or paid attention better to the instruction he received. The arm-waving amplification of his leader probably helped. There were all sorts of possibilities as to why there was a different result the second time around.

The snow had not yet ended for the hikers, but the trail was closer to trees below them than they'd made it the day before. Colton tended to take a look at the trees down the mountain and anticipate a slide. Oh, he was still interested in the adventure, but he was less willing to be uncalculating, preferring a less dramatic experience. That said, trying to control an accident versus focusing on the avoidance of said occurrence are two different approaches. Avoidance should work better, wouldn't you think? But this was Col.

The turn toward the west (or down the mountain a bit) came, and all of a sudden, there were people. Humans! There were two guys and two girls. All were younger than our guys. Likely much younger. Or they appeared to be, anyway. At least much younger than Col. None of the four appeared to be carrying chainsaws or big knives or other weapons. No one was dressed all in pink. So, it appeared to be safe enough for the new campers, on first analysis. Colton was thinking too much. That, or he had watched too many horror movies.

The six of them chatted for several minutes. The four were headed to the boulder shelter – not the place on top of the ridge, but another place on past Home Lake for some hiking in that general direction. Col thought that he and Bill had been through there (and they had). The foursome had come from somewhere east of Marmot Pass and had ventured down to the Dosewallips River and Camp Deception to spend the prior night, but they had not gone, nor did they plan to go, any farther. They had not seen anyone until Bill and Col and had no information about Deception Basin. None of the four had a lot of experience climbing rocks or mountains. No technical expertise, that is. Without the benefit of his notes, Colton could not remember much more about them – like their names – but all were from the Tacoma area, if he remembered that part correctly. Colton did recall their sense of humor when everyone introduced themselves – one of the guys said to him, "Were you on a poster campaign at Rainier about twenty years ago?" *Very funny*. Colt admitted he had seen the posters that the hiker was speaking of.

They also had a cousin named Colton who they always kidded about that.

After a few minutes, off they went up toward the ridge and the snowfields. Bill and Colton continued the other direction. Despite the opportunity to tell his story, Colt did not mention slip-sliding away down the mountain. The poster reference had made Colton think that that was just not the right time to describe a personal failing in the mountains, and thus validating the use of his name. And, he also had to explain the posters to Bill.

Chapter Sixteen

Down to the River and Back

⟩—┼┼———⟩

"DON'T BE LIKE COLTON!" The posters were in the Mount Rainier Welcome Center, or whatever the facility was called, up towards the mountain. Bill did not recall them, but he believed the city boy's recounting of them. *Why would he make something like that up?*

"Sounds like they found as their example a guy with the perfect name," Bill noted and smiled.

"My first wife used to say something like, 'No, I don't like macaroni salad', or something like that," Colt replied.

"What has that got to do with anything?"

"It was her way to change the subject," Colt replied.

It seems to this narrator that Bill may have found a quasi-sensitive issue for his old friend.

Then Colt chuckled. "No, had not thought about those posters for years until flying out here this time, trying to recall my prior visits. That was funny. Can't recall what they had the caricature of that Colton wearing."

"Maybe a black T-shirt and gray shorts," Bill offered.

"Hey," Col, who happened to be wearing that combination at the time (and throughout the hike – no change of clothes in the backpack, remember?), answered.

Bill laughed.

Bill and Colton soon left the trail through a break in the trees, generally following the openness above them, which was to their right and forward. This area was more open, with fewer trees. They came upon an even thinner forested area where they could move more easily than through the rough and thicker woods that had been more prominent at many points so far in their journey. Bill thought the route taken might result in them being lower than some might prefer, but it was safer in other regards with a modest ascent to the meadow.

The air was filled with what Colton identified as a pine scent. (He learned later that it was really more cedar-like.) And there didn't seem to be too much of a wetness to the air, although, it wasn't dry either. There was also a hint of flowers, which grew stronger as they continued.

They made the first leg of their off-trail journey successfully. No falls. No drama. They broke into a clearer area, with more rocks, and then through another thinner area of trees above the thicker woods below. There was less snow, but still at times, the footwork was tricky, like an uneven floor with obstacles.

And then they were there – in an expanse of land void of trees and with just a few shrubs, very different from anything they had encountered up to that point, especially the size of the area. They had succeeded in finding Sunnybrook Meadow! The beautiful area was not lost!

"This flowering one is lupine," Bill said, beginning to point out some of the vegetation. "It's all over the place, as you can see. That white flowering one is cow-parsnip. You may not want to roll around in it, but casual contact may not hurt."

"So, are there cows?" Col asked.

"No, just the parsnip. Now, this taller plant or grass is bear grass. Do you want to ask about …"

"No. I'm sure it's just a name for the grass," Colton stated, while at the same time sniffing ... nope, he could not smell his blood … that was good.

"Well, bears do eat this if they are around the grass, but they don't have to be where the grass is to survive," Bill explained. "And here are more flowers – elephant head, some bog orchids. Smell those."

"Okay, but I have a terrible recognition of scents … is that vanilla?"

"Yep. You got that one, Col," Bill said and grinned.

"I'm somewhat stunned at recognizing that," Col said, kind of tickled he got one right.

As they wandered around, continuing with plant introductions, they realized they had a dilemma of sorts. Just a timing issue, but one they would need to resolve. They thought they were still too far from the next preferred campsite, yet there seemed like there was a reasonable quantity of daylight left – could be a lot left, they weren't exactly sure. They did not have a frisbee, so that was out. Too much additional weight for the backpack, you know. And there were no cow pies to serve as frisbees, not that you would even try to catch those. Some people might try to throw them, though. There were no cows, remember? Just the parsnip.

They could go to the Deception Creek campsite, where the Tacoma area foursome had spent the night prior, and then up about 3,000 feet to the right or kind of go east from there to Deception Basin. Once at that point, the mountaineering effort might need to kick in – especially with the snow that could be reasonably expected after all the lower snow they had seen so far which wasn't really expected. There would be hidden crevices and deep snow in spots. Ice was almost certain.

Exciting stuff!

Bill would be alright with his training-obtained approach. Colton? Not so much. There might be a lesser of multiple evils if they proceeded through the meadow and toward Royal Basin, reducing some of the potential problems. Who knew? Honestly, Colt was no "technical climber" in any regard. He wasn't a rock climber either. Bill knew there would be a path or two over to Royal Basin that would not require full "technical" expertise (or training), but the snow depth might cause just as many issues or even end up making the task "technical" or, at least a lot more difficult. That would depend on the amount of ice as well as the depth of the snow. The decision whether or not to go over the ridge could not be answered without getting there, but they did not want to get there and then have to turn around.

There was another route available through a "pass" of sorts north of Mount Fricaba, reached via Milk Creek or a second path or trail in that direction. That meant going back by Home Lake and then up, past Fricaba. On the other side would be the Royal Basin. That was not in Bill's previous itineraries through the area to get over to Royal Lake, but it might work, and he knew there had to be a way through there.

Decisions, decisions …

"Let's at least head down to see the river or get close enough to hear the water," Colt suggested.

Bill agreed and liked the sense of adventure coming from Colt.

The journey before them to the turn in the trail was about a three and a third mile round trip, kind of northwest, above the river, after a 3,200-foot descent, and the return climb to the meadow. *Golly*. Several hours' worth of effort. They could add another mile or so and head over toward the Twin Creeks area. That was relatively flat, as Bill remembered, and offered a lot easier, even quicker, hiking. They would see when they arrived at the turn how they felt and how high the sun was. That might be their decision point, as there were camping sites down that direction, like Deception Creek, although the meadow seemed like a great campsite, and Deception Creek was some distance past the twin creeks.

The trail down was great. Easy to navigate. There were switchbacks to enable a clean hike versus a downhill scoot. Of course, it was still quite the angle downhill, but there were no falls. No spills. No long sliding maneuvers. It was a nice, safe hike. Col was beginning to appreciate what Bill had said once about descents being more accident prone than ascents. You don't slip upwards, he'd said.

At the trail turning point to follow along above the river, they might have caught a glimpse of the river through the trees. They had seen the river somewhat better a couple of times from farther up the mountain, but they were much closer now. And … they could make out the sound of the river.

Bill commented on the water appearing to be a tad cloudy, but he was not sure without a real solid look. That would usually mean the water level was a little higher, he explained.

With a little more than a mile to wander to the twin creeks, they decided to do so, as there still seemed to be a lot of daylight remaining. It would be a nice extension to their hike. And it would be pretty flat, according to Bill's recollection. And he was correct. There was also a nice waterfall above the twins. A bonus!

Colton was thinking that, at some point, he would regard the modesty of Bill's memory as a way to increase his excitement versus feeding any doubts he had. Bill had been there. He knew the place. Weather, the amount of daylight, and all kinds of other factors make every hike, even over the same area, a new adventure. Just like Trail 2 at Shades. Every single time that trail was joyous for Col, as the Olympic hikes were likely that for Bill, every time.

Once they were near the creeks, the decision was made to ease back up to the meadow versus trekking any further. The trail did not really get much closer to the river than at Twin Creeks, as the river appeared to come more from the northwest and the trail more north, widening the gap between the river and the trail. Back to the meadow meant going up yet again and a fair distance to go from the creeks. Even if they decided to return that way and chance the possibility of the snow impact in the basin, that meadow seemed like a tremendous place to spend the night.

The repeat hike down would be fine. Every hike was a new experience. Of course, going on to the next campsite could probably have been achieved that day. Continuing on to the basin seemed to have been already ruled out in Bill's mind. And rightfully so, Colt thought. There were too many questions unanswered.

The return up the mountain really wasn't that bad, if taken at a fair pace. So, that's what they did. They didn't need to rush, as they expected there to be enough daylight left to easily reach a camping site in plenty of time to have dinner (oh, exciting – noodles?) and set up for the night.

The switchbacks helped level the effect somewhat. The views, as with coming down, were beautiful but seemed more appreciated while going up – those long pauses taken to gather yourself, catch your breath, rest your legs, and see the sights, all were perfect moments for a deeper appreciation of your surroundings.

Colton's knee seemed to be doing surprisingly well. It was a little achy, but not enough to complain about. Course, there was no one to appreciate his complaint (not that Bill was totally without empathy or sympathy or something), and there was a nightly break coming up reasonably soon anyway. Colt did not want to appear exceptionally wimpish, so there was that fact, too.

That extension was a wonderful down and back hike. Therefore, Colt was glad they didn't have a frisbee … or cow pies.

The time had arrived once more to relax. It was chill time in the meadow. The designated camping area was among trees – some fir and cedar. The air was filled with the evergreen scent of the fir trees (or so Col thought) and there was also that unmistakable cedar smell as well. The occasional black fly or mosquito was around – Bill noted that the air temperature and excess snow could have kept the population down some that year. The tree fragrances, though, and the flowers made the place a great place to camp and gave Colton's knee the opportunity to rest just a little bit more. It might stiffen up. Might not. There was no internet to look up "How to build a sled". And there was no book on the topic in their possession (too much weight to be carried). All was very well, though.

Chapter Seventeen

Options (Except for Oatmeal and Noodles)

The tents "popped" open for a fourth night of leisure out in the forest, out in the wild, somewhere in Washington. They were out of wine as far as Colton knew, not that he asked, as he was doing just fine with the purified water. And, they still had noodles and oatmeal. Plus the energy bars – but, they were saving those for a rest while heading up a mountain. or a restful stop where said bars seemed earned.

The deep scratches on Colton's leg were coagulated. Basically, they were pretty well scabbed for the most part. There were no open wounds, no dripping blood. The fear of a bear's smelling capability had been significantly reduced. The back of Colton's mind had been busy with other issues to consider more seriously.

"Should we tuck away some bear grass in the event we run into Boo-Boo or Yogi or Cindy Bear?" the mildly hobbled Colton inquired.

"No. You likely don't want to be close enough to offer them a snack. Plus, if that close, you might look more appetizing, at least to a bear with no cultural upbringing on fine food. Doubt it, but you never know…," Bill responded.

"Well, I certainly do not want to appear too tempting," Col said, deciding that was enough of that conversation.

In addition to mulling over the options for the following day and the possible food interests of hungry bears, there was another opportunity to chat more about life. Or lives. Two lives. Colton was on marriage number three, a record tending not to support a second career in marriage counseling should his current career evaporate and the opportunity arise. At least some of what not to do may have made an impression, and thus could be good counsel, but maybe not. *Guess he was a slow learner.* Could Col write a book entitled "How Not to be Married?" Or something like that. Perhaps. You would think he had wise things to consider as far as not doing this or that and then doing others. Colton said that one of his medical directors once said he wished he'd thought of the thoughtful, romantic things that Colton used to do. Col's efforts may have been faulty in their delivery. Or maybe Col's misunderstanding of entire situations could have been the real issues. He wasn't sure. He saw the symbolic nature of words (not poetic, necessarily) and gestures. At times. Other times, no, he completely missed the mark or, at least, any comprehension of what the marks actually were.

Bill had never been married. He had rented the same "bachelor apartment", as he called his place, for years in Seattle. Colton suggested that he could end up meeting a nice Indiana University girl someday and settle down – not that Bill was overly rambunctious and was interested in/required "settling".

Colton had two daughters and a stepson and stepdaughter. Bill had no children. The discussion on children led Col to comment on his feeling that "stepchildren" remained your stepchildren forever, even if the marriage failed. The status of "children" does not change with the state of matrimony was his point. *Seemed like a very reasonable position.*

Bill had a lot of family back east. Colton, too. Different parts of the "east", but in that general direction. Colton's were primarily in Indiana; Bill's in the New England and northeast area. Colton did have a sister who lived west of the Mississippi, but all his other siblings, plus most of his cousins and many other relatives, were still Hoosiers.

Both men had essentially the same or similar careers. The management of people. Officers in corporations. They didn't work for themselves. They studied and made decisions relating to risk – life insurance risk. Underwriting. Risk decisions were every bit of the work they encountered. Training people how to do that job well was also in their job descriptions. Creating guidelines that would fit actuarial assumptions on the mortality of a life insurance product. *Exciting stuff.* Not as exciting as falling down a mountain, possibly, but that could very well be a risk to calculate.

They both had experience considering risks for people who chose to hang out among the mountains. Colton recalled one case where the proposed insured was an ice climber in Canada, but he couldn't remember where he lived when he wasn't scaling ice. Colton could not recall how the case – one such case in forty some years – was handled or what decision was made on the assumption of risk. How much more would a person pay for life insurance who did the ice climbing only annually? The real question was: How much is the appropriate charge for the risk associated with that once-a-year adventure? Colton could not recall the decision.

"That's why underwriting manuals are in writing or on-line, so you can look up the risk – you don't have to memorize everything," Colton stated.

Underwriting manuals are usually produced by companies that assist life insurance companies with risk coverage and analysis, if not produced by the company itself, and they include opinions on risks and how significant the risks might be to the life expectancy of the one seeking insurance coverage. Since not any two risks (or people) are exactly alike, there are a myriad of differences that complicate, but also help define, the overall risk. Theoretically, every risk has numerous complexities, but a very large percentage of people fall into the largest class where distinctions are not so narrowly made. Not every risk could possibly be covered by the manuals, so good collaboration with experts across the industry was an excellent strategy to assist in making prudent decisions.

Despite his personal interest, Bill could not recall having a "mountain climber" as a risk to evaluate. He had people that did some "rock climbing", but that's a bit different – could be better or worse than those mountain climbing. Depends on the rocks and the scale, which is a score for the difficulty of the climb. The risks he saw were not terribly difficult – no one was scaling El Capitan or some of the other more difficult rock faces. Still, many were complicated risks to evaluate. Claiming to be a rock climber and being a true technical rock climber are a little different, too. Most people who hike any, at all, likely climb through rocks at times, but they are not "rock climbers".

And that was a nice segue to the question then before them: Should they make another visit to the Dosewallips River and then an adventure forth to near Mount Deception from the west and on to Royal Basin or make a visit to Constance Pass again to try getting to the basin from the other direction?

Going the river route and then up to Deception Basin, between Mount Deception and Mount Mystery, might lead to turning around and coming back through the river trail, the meadow area, the ridge, the pass, by Home Lake and then towards the car. The decision might be based on the snow levels in Deception Basin, as well as finding the less difficult path for the city boy through the area. Bill had been that way and knew there were acceptable options that Colton really could manage without any extra training or experience. And Bill was not inclined to place his buddy at any great risk of injury or death. He still thought there were options IF the conditions were right. The snow so far suggested that conditions might not be perfect for, at least, even close to the normal ones he had experienced in prior adventures through the area. So, he was concerned about that.

Going the creek (or an alternative) route up towards what might be a pass of sorts north of Mount Fricaba meant doing all the backtracking first (except not all the way back to the car) and then potentially backing up from the "pass" to the original route and back, possibly approaching Royal Lake from the Dungeness River side, if there was time (and there might be). The big question again would be the snow in that area north of the peak and the level of difficulty required to make the transition to the basin. Bill did not have personal experience for that particular pass, but he knew the general area.

What to do, what to do …

Colt had already demonstrated his uncanny skills of handling a walk in the snow (at least the second attempt was much better, after the additional coaching). That seemed more of an issue heading toward the river route, but it could also come into play the creek route. They would not know until they arrived at either.

After a dinner of – you guessed it – noodles (there were absolutely no options other than that; nothing could take its place; nothing else for dinner for Colton in mountain life), the guys decided to make the final call in the morning.

The setting of the sun and rising of the moon were slightly different that night, less spectacular than two nights before, but still pretty impressive. They were more on the side of the mountain than on a ridge, yet it was "reasonably" flat, so the view was still great.

Their tents were soon up. All their chores were completed. And their sleeping bags were filled. All was well in their world for another night in the wild.

Chapter Eighteen

Bears Don't Bleat

No cell service and no watch kind of left them guessing about the hour. So, the time could have been 3:00 a.m., or not, but it seemed as good a guess as any (it was 3:00 a.m. somewhere…), regardless, there was activity outside their tents.

Colton heard snorting, not as loud as elk, and there was also some other kind of noise, like bleating from a sheep. (The city boy didn't really know what the sound was except he thought sheep made the kind of crying noise he thought he was hearing.) The critter appeared to be eating. Col didn't hear Bill screaming, so the animal likely wasn't munching on Bill. And the sound wasn't one Colton would expect from a bear, but he remained quiet anyway, not willing to draw unnecessary attention to himself.

This apparent vegetarian either very slowly moved on through their camp or else Colton didn't fall asleep as fast as with the elk the night before. Whichever, the latest critter visit seemed to take a while. Eventually, though, sleep once again came.

And with rest, the time came to greet a new day. As breakfast was being prepared, Bill anticipated Colton's question.

"Mountain goat," he said.

"What kind of sound was that exactly?" Colton asked, not being even close to being an expert on the subject.

"Well, they supposedly make a sound called a bleat, but I'm not going to imitate it. And I think usually they just kind of snort. Never heard a bleat myself. Not sure I heard one last night."

Colt tried to make a bleat.

"Close enough," Bill said. "But, let's not do it again."

Could be that Bill confused Col's attempt to "bleat" as him trying to sing. Having not lived through Colton singing yet, he was more than likely confused by the sounds being made. *Rightfully so.*

Colt was glad bears did not bleat. And yes, he was glad they had not been visited by a bear. Years later, Bill talked again about the mountain goats – authorities apparently were trying to remove many of them from some areas they were in as they were not native and were being a little too destructive. Not sure how they gathered them up, but they gave it a whirl. Bill said he would have to get back out there and check on them. (A report on the national park website reported over 400 were removed from 2018 through 2020, with most being transported to the Cascades, where they were native.)

"The advantage to the internet is that you can hear the sound too. Can't do that in a dictionary," Colton offered. "I'm still as glad for dictionaries as underwriting manuals … I just have trouble spelling some words."

Bill thought he himself was an acceptable speller.

Colt noted, "Of course, if you cannot spell a word, how are you going to look it up in a dictionary?"

"Excellent observation, Professor," Bill retorted. "Very true."

Colt then went on to describe the only example he could think of at that moment where he had had trouble spelling and that was "rapport". He finally found the word and learned its spelling. He wasn't sure why he didn't know the spelling to begin with, but his search had taken a bit of time to complete. It wasn't a "w" word (wrap versus rap, for example), and then there were those two "p's". (Education is a wonderful thing. But luck is also sometimes wonderful as well, isn't it?)

Word Play finished for the moment, over the morning ritual of oatmeal, the guys then moved on to discuss the options for the day's journey. There were options aplenty, but at least two general approaches needed to be seriously considered. Not knowing the weather conditions – specifically, the snow

accumulation or lack of snow melt being the major concerns –
left them really guessing.

The exciting route, as far as the scenery and mountains and
so forth, would seem to be going the river route and then up to
the Deception Basin. It would be more original territory to
conquer or at least explore. There would be a variety of nature
to enjoy – trees, rivers, snow, mountains, etc. The change in
elevation would be huge – about 3,500 feet or thereabouts in two
directions – but they had done much of that the day prior.
Arguably, it was a net of near zero feet, as they would go down
about that many feet and then up again the same general
distance. "Net zero" makes their task at hand sound easier, right?
But it wasn't that way, really, it was just a Colt mathematical
thing. The almost-an-actuary coming out in him. Or actuary-
want-to-be.

They had already explored the way down toward the river
and on to the twin creeks. Seems like that route would also be
steeper when going back up to Deception Basin, but that was
uncertain. There would be hard work, but Colton didn't mind
that. It was the fact that the effort required could possibly be just
a little outside his skill set on the technical side once they arrived
in that basin. Hard to say, though. Again, Bill knew there would
be Colton-esque routes up there under "normal" conditions, but
the snow could be a significant factor influencing the current
definition of normality, and it could very well make some of
their options obscure. The higher the elevation, the more likely
the snow issue would develop. So, there was that to consider too.

The "haven't we been here before" passage would pass the
commode – not that this was vitally important now – but it might
also give them a slightly better chance to actually get to the

Royal Basin and the Royal Lake Trail. The "slightly" needs to be emphasized. There was still the chance that their course would hit a wall. But there was also the distinct possibility of a great adventure. This one also had varied natural settings with possibly less snow since there was a somewhat lower elevation.

There was discussion on the options. No debate, mind you, as Colton did not know enough to present a case one way or the other, although he may have interjected an opinion here or there. The discussion was more of a description of Bill's past treks through the areas under consideration. The choice was made to try the Milk Creek, or an alternative route in that general direction, to attempt passage from the Mount Fricaba area toward Royal Lake. They wouldn't know until they arrived, but the snow cover already being worse than expected seemed to suggest that Deception Basin could be really treacherous, and more than the city boy could handle.

There is truth to the perception that going in the opposite direction is, indeed, a new route. And, as stated earlier, there is truth to the fact that every hike, even on the same trail in the same direction, is a different window on the world. The already repeated route, though, would be from the site of the infamous downhill slide to Home Lake – hopefully, they would avoid the icy hill or glacier and take a side path or, even better, the actual trail. Colton wondered if the actual trail even went through the glacier. They would essentially be on the same trail or path until the cutoff was made toward the pass, whose name wasn't known or didn't exist. The two could try to name the pass. "Pass with No Name" sounded reasonable.

There was no particular objective for Night Five as far as a resting place. Not as in their "final resting place", but rather just one for that night. The friends agreed that most anything would work. There would be plenty of options, and they could just stop when they wanted to, pretty much – even at an unofficial camping location, outside of the national park itself.

There was one absolute truth on their journey that day: their surroundings were beautiful.

"I have another Rumi quote," Bill offered. "'Beauty surrounds us, but usually we need to be walking in a garden to know it.'"

"Truth," Col responded. "All of us likely have those moments where we get caught up in life and miss what is around us. We just have to stop and look. Many times, we don't look close enough, though."

"It's too easy to be too busy, or something, and miss the good life surrounding you."

"Myna, my younger dog, has always stopped to smell the flowers. My thought, given her sense of smell, was that had to be a huge rush, but she's always done that. Appreciates flowers, I guess," Colt said.

"Now that doesn't seem to be a regular trait of a dog," Bill responded.

"Nope. True, though."

Even for the third time, the "area of loose footing" view, looking out across the land, both up and down the mountain, was magnificent! That could be a good name for the big patch of snow – "the area of loose footing". Colton did not want his name on it, though. Might end up in another ad campaign of "DON'T BE LIKE COLTON!"

They did not visit the bloody pine and the pile of dead limbs or the launching pad. They stayed higher above, looking down, enabling another slip, if it should happen, to go just a bit farther down the side of the mountain. Well, they joked about that possibility. But being earlier in the day, the snow was not yet reacting quite as much to the sun. So, they were a wee bit safer. You would think the air temperature would eat away at the snow as well, but that doesn't seem to have the same impact. (This presents an opportunity for a scientific comment, but, no, let's move on, shall we?)

Chapter Nineteen

Noodle Soup or, Perhaps, Stew …

Despite the return to Constance Pass, there was still something new about the scene. The different time of day, different light, different direction, different shadows – there was just, again, a change that made the journey unique, while they were still able to recognize some of the prominent features from their past visits. Colton thought back to Shades State Park (again) – they always seemed to take Trail 2, every single time, and yet every time, the odyssey seemed new or, at least, just as exciting.

Opening your eyes to the beauty around you reduces that "been there, done that" state of mind. There was no "seen one trail, you've seen them all" mentality, either. Colton was sad for people who might feel that way. In fact, if you've seen one trail, you'll never see that path the same way again. Period. And that point Colton made over and over again as they discussed all their experiences. Being older allowed him the luxury of repeating himself some.

For the second time on their trek, there was only evidence of humans as they wandered by several tents very near where they had spent Night Two. But there were no people. No marmots this time – or goats. The tents were different colors, different types than the first they saw. (The location was where Bill recalled he had seen mountain goats on one trip he took a few years before.) These folk were not climbers, apparently, as the tents were not in the rock shelter.

One good note about humans: the guys had not seen any trash left behind. *Good humans.*

The four they met from Tacoma were headed the direction Colton and Bill were going, but that was about a day ago, and their destination was a whole lot farther. Colton and Bill chatted about the benefit or lack thereof of setting up the tents and then just wandering around the countryside. They seemed to agree that the best approach would be to lug the forty pounds around in their backpacks until they were done for the day, allowing them to keep in pursuit of the next great piece of nature they could find to camp amidst.

The pass, named Constance, definitely seemed brighter this time around. The view was expansive.

The view made Colton remember his first time on Trail Ridge Road in Rocky Mountain National Park and the surrounding area. He recalled taking over 250 pictures. Every turn, every angle, every mountain was unique and needed documentation in the form of a photograph. Constance Pass was stunning! Unfortunately, he didn't have a camera, though, so there would be no evidence except in his mind's eye.

The 250 pictures from RMNP were kind of a joke to everyone. Once printed, no one could really differentiate where most of them had been taken, not that all the mountains and so forth looked the same. Obviously, something made the photographer think, "WOW!" But back in the 70's, you had to print the negatives. There was no digital camera to screen and edit and no GPS record of where they were taken … at least there were none that Colt could afford. There was no time or GPS stamp. The next time he was in the Olympics (if there was a next time), Col decided right then and there that he would bring a battery charger – a solar one would be best – so there could be pictures taken.

As they made their way wide of Home Lake, avoiding the glacier, Bill started reminiscing about taking a dive into the lake for "cleansing purposes". Colt, being a non-swimmer, could get his legs and arms clean. Bill also recalled prior treks through the general area, including what was to come in the Royal Lake area. Then, he thought of visiting Goat Lake, almost 6,000 feet above sea level. And a lightbulb popped on in his head …

He imagined that a Goat Lake approach might be a better alternative route to getting over to Royal Basin. He described the possibility to Colton as pretty much going back to where they stayed the first night and turning left – not exactly, but close enough. The turn itself would not get them to Goat Lake or Royal Basin, but the adventure would be in that basic direction, just up another mountain and across another ridge.

Bill remembered that the way over the mountains there did not seem terribly steep the entire route, but it was exciting. He had never taken the route from the Dungeness River side, the way they would be approaching, but he had come over from the Royal Basin side to Goat Lake, the opposite direction, at least a couple of times. He wasn't even sure there was a great route that way. Hikers were on their own. Creativity required.

He also mentioned that there was no established trail above Goat Lake to or from Royal Lake, either. He pictured a sparse bivy spot not far below the ridge above Goat Lake. That would be a camping option to consider if they stopped short of Royal Lake. There was ready water around the lake – an important consideration for any camping spot, temporary or not – and a fine sunrise view.

Col experienced a new word in that discussion – "bivy" – which he learned was a temporary or improvised campsite, formally named a "bivouac shelter".

Bill shared the first time he came through there, up from near Royal Lake. His climbing pal, Barry, had exclaimed, upon seeing the approximate 1,500 foot "grunt" (as he called the climb) they had to deal with, "That's the worst jumble of boulders I've ever seen." Bill was certain his actual utterance was more colorful, but the point was that there was quite the maze of car-sized boulders on the west, or Royal Lake side, that you had to navigate while climbing the steep, west-facing slope, under a full pack. They did that particular hike in the late afternoon sun. Both times he had gone that way, he explained, the correct route somehow seemed intuitive – at least from the west. But now, he and Colt would face the obstacles from the other direction.

"One of the things I enjoy most about cross-country travel is route finding," Bill added.

That made Colt think that Bill could be an interesting travel guide for more adventures. If time wasn't a serious consideration, he basically kind of took any given route one step at a time. He would find the path, and then, smell it out.

Their trek might be slow. And their quest could be a little steep. But they agreed to take a look. At least they could see another mountain lake while exploring. And that would make for a better time.

The trip down Constance Pass this time was pretty uneventful. Still not the easiest trail, but it was void of the pitfalls through the trees and over the ice. As they made their way along, Colton asked about snakes. They had not seen any. Colton was not a big fan, as we know, and he had not even thought about them (for at least a few minutes), but a glance to the ground on his left made him think of snakes – there was a branch that was "snake-shaped". Bill was not sure that there were reptiles of any kind that high in elevation (over 5,000 feet), but also there were no venomous snakes or lizards or anything akin to them in the general area, including the whole Washington peninsula and its Olympic Mountains. The comfort of not having to worry about venomous varieties, like he did while hiking back east in south central Indiana, allowed Colton to focus on bears and other creatures. (He also didn't have to worry about bears back east in Indiana parks. No mountain goats or cougars, either. Nor marmots. There were bobcats that sometimes were a little bigger than one might expect, but they hid very well, and he had never seen one – and bobcats weren't cougars or mountain lions.)

The concerning snakes back home were the copperhead, a particularly unpleasant sort, not inclined to appreciate a human at all, even if one were being kind to it, and the timber rattlesnake, more the kind to avoid you and slither away as long as you didn't corner or mess with it. You shouldn't let your dog try to make friends with them, either. If you go into Northern Indiana, you might also find an eastern massasauga rattlesnake – pretty shy swamp dweller – or if you go to the southwestern corner of Indiana, near the Ohio River, you might find a cottonmouth (or water moccasin). Once Colton learned that the dogs of friends in the Indiana woods had survived copperhead bites, he relaxed quite a bit about his home there with his dogs.

But back to Colt's current adventure …

Bill didn't seem too terribly concerned about bears. They were around, but not common to the spot they were in. He then mentioned what he thought was a fact about Olympic National Park: mountain goats had killed more people than black bears. That might be true, might not, but it was definitely an attempt to soothe any concerns Colton had about bears, which he appreciated.

Now he could just worry about the goats.

Bill did not recall ever seeing a bear in the wild while on a hike around where they were near Home Lake. Elsewhere on the hikes, yes. Colton said he had not seen one in the wild, but then he recalled seeing one in Michigan once, in the UP (or the Upper Peninsula). That was his only experience – and the bear was way off in the distance, across a field near a tree line that Colton was driving by. The beasts are big and stand out – hard to miss them, even the smaller ones, in case you wanted to know.

Colton broke the bear moments with his question of the day: "What's for dinner?"

"Marmot noodle soup," came the reply from his friend. "I've heard marmot tastes like chicken."

"Never have seen chickens in the wild," Colton claimed, "except in Key West."

Bill thought a moment and then replied, "I suppose Key West can be considered wild."

"At times, Key West is wild. Like New Year's. And their Halloween celebration. Chickens do fly. I was in a heavenly restaurant once in Key West with outside tables covered by umbrellas, and a chicken flew down from a tree and hit the umbrella. Maybe they don't fly very well. As God is my witness, I do know turkeys don't fly."

"Different knowledge than some radio station managers," Bill offered.

"And a great episode," Colton added. "Did you know there was a real WKRP station? The call letters were used by a station near North Vernon, Indiana, if I remember correctly. And I think you could, with a good antenna, hear the station in Cincinnati. There might have been other stations that used those letters."

For a change, Colt educated Bill. Sort of.

By the way, there was no marmot enhancement of the noodles that night. There would be another time to compare marmot with chicken – or not – but not that night. They didn't have a marmot hunting license, not that there was such a thing. Although, as for all Colt knew, it could be a requirement, though it probably wasn't permitted at all in the national park. Whichever the case, they decided not to risk arrest on marmot hunting out of season.

The trail did not look familiar at all, but it was the same trail they had trekked a couple or so days earlier in the opposite direction. As you know, it made sense that the route would seem a little different. They were not making sixteen to seventeen miles a day, as the very first person to complete the Appalachian Trail claimed he did, but this was also not the Appalachians.

They had been on several trails over their journey heading into Night Five. The adventure was a wander in the forest of sorts. At least they weren't lost. That hadn't crossed their minds because Bill knew the area well, and Colt trusted Bill. He even trusted him when he withheld information, such as the recent bear scat he had noticed – a steaming one, with berries – as they ventured on (which he didn't tell Colton until later … much later).

While Bill had seen and was impressed by a Goat Lake sunrise, that seemed out of the question for the next morning. It was too far to travel before dark. Though, Col might pick up the pace some and quit pausing for storytelling. Regardless, the time had come to consider their hike finished for the day.

The guys decided on a spot for the night that was not as awe-inspiring as some of the other nights had been. It was more in the denseness of the forest, not really near what would necessarily be considered a "camp". That was in part because they were not exactly sure where they were. No, they weren't lost. They knew they were near the Pacific Northwest Trail group of trails – meaning they were within a quarter of a mile or so of the trail that was likely higher than where they were. Bill knew they were headed in the right direction as they were following the creek (versus a trail).

Bill was also pretty sure they were no longer in the national park. In the park, you could not "boondock" or camp anywhere you wanted to. You needed a reservation at an approved campsite. In the national forest, there was real, primitive camping (not at a campsite, and even boondocking), without running afoul of the law. So, if they weren't within the national park boundaries, they were good; and if they were, well, a ranger wandering through at night might apprehend them as criminals. Bill knew they were really close to the park border, but he was "99% sure" they were beyond the line. They decided to chance a random ranger discovery in the dark of night. They did not plan to build a fire, which eliminated another possible violation.

They were beside a creek again, like they were the first night, but this was not as thrilling a site in Col's mind. This creek, Home Creek, a somewhat quieter creek. Bill thought they weren't too far from where Home Creek and Heather Creek come together to form the Dungeness River, which was definitely outside the park. Still, they were in the wild, the wilderness. And that was potentially exciting. They could run into marmots again, although they had agreed they were not equipped to be hunters and didn't have the license. That was enough of a deterrent (if they needed one). Is there a marmot hunting season? They didn't know. But they didn't want to risk being caught violating that law, either. Probably not the same offense as littering, but still on the rap sheet, nonetheless.

Chapter Twenty

No Ritz to Put On

Night Five was also a "noodle night" – matching nights one through four. *Exciting.* A pattern that had become a rut of sorts.

"I was thinking of marmot hunting as something on a rap sheet, which made me think of littering, which made me think of *Alice's Restaurant*. You know that song, Bill?"

"I recall blind justice. And – where were the criminals – on a bench? The W4 bench? That song you could actually sing, Col, because most is narration, except for the part about getting anything you want at the restaurant."

"Maybe marmot," Colt replied.

"Perhaps," Bill agreed. "Maybe take-out only, though."

"As far as encounters with the protectors of the environment, my only opportunity was on a pontoon boat on a lake in mid-Michigan. That was the county sheriff, not the DNR, and their mission was to enforce boating regulations. So, they stopped us. Counted the people on board. Then they asked to see the life jackets. We had enough, as well as a round life ring and even some other sort of floatation device. We also had flares. I don't think they gave a 'get-out-of-a-ticket card' for any of that, though. Instead, they did write tickets and escorted you to a dock – no 'I'll have it on me next time' rationale to stay out on the lake. They also looked at boat registration and so forth. Nice people to the law-abiding, and we were that day."

"Never had a ranger out here stop and check anything. They could be too busy helping those who cannot help themselves or those that run into trouble, quite by accident, despite plenty of experience and knowledge. And they aren't going to be wandering the woods at night, either."

Dinner went as well as a fifth straight night of noodles could go. Their tents opened as expected. The air seemed moister than some places they had been, but it wasn't particularly humid. They were more closed in with the creek and in thicker trees. The temperature was unknown, but it wasn't hot, by any means. Night began to fall in a little darker than it had done on the prior nights. Sleep was chasing them a wee bit quicker. And it came before the darkness had completely enveloped their camp.

But there was no sleep to be had, for long – they had company. And this wasn't a marmot or an elk or a goat.

Bill had never encountered a bear camping in that particular area of the Olympic National Forest. Colton had seen bears in zoos – oh, and in the UP, from a distance. Now, they had a chance to properly introduce themselves. "Bear, Bill … Bill, Bear…" That did not seem to be the time for Bill to mention the steaming pile of scat he had failed to point out to Colton earlier in the evening.

The bear, apparently on his (or her) own, which is fairly normal, although hopefully, he/she was not doing reconnaissance for a sleuth of bears (at least it wasn't a band of mountain goats – goats are indeed killers), was just kind of moseying along. It was not exceptionally large, but large enough to make "bagging it" a huge quest. They had done all the right things with their food and such. And they were hoping they didn't have a noodle-loving bear to deal with, who might have a refined nose for noodles.

Not doing anything that could be positively identified as aggressive, the black bear was just poking around, not appearing to be interested in the tents too much, rather simply meandering through along the creek. Colton would have given up his tent, if necessary, but that appeared not to be of concern. They had no pots or pans to clang … well … they did have a pan. One pan. They could beat that one pan against the frame of the heater or cooking device. Colton was just hoping he wouldn't need a change of pants – because remember, he didn't have any. Nor did he have extra underwear, and it might require more than just a positional shift of the underwear, as described earlier, if he were to be significantly frightened. Luckily, they still had plenty of toilet paper.

Bill and Col had their tents closer together than the previous nights. So, if they needed to scare the bear, they could get together to appear larger – well, a taller guy with a shorter sidekick, so not much larger, but a little bit anyway. Might be entertaining for the bear. They had no top hats, canes, or music. No putting on the ritz. Colton should probably avoid singing – they certainly didn't want to anger the potential monster.

The guys could barely see each other, and Colton – who wasn't crying yet – was trying to look for any indication from Bill of a need to do anything. Being in their respective tents, he could not really see Bill anyway, so it was each man for himself.

They were both watchful for the time being. Watching the bear. There was no discussion. No talking. No yelling. No crying. Colton thought that doing nothing was better than doing anything that could be misinterpreted as aggressive to said visitor.

There was nothing for the bear to smell in the open as far as noodles. Or oatmeal. If he or she had been tailing the guys, the bear might not have survived until the fifth night, thinking, "Noodles again?!" Doubt the bear had been listening and heard and understood their earlier marmot talk. The bear apparently had not been on their trail. In addition to the noodle query, the bear might have thought with all the back-and-forth movement that the guys were really lost.

The beast wandered closer to Colt's tent, still outside of the tents, and closer to the water. The thought of extra clothes as a potential requirement again flashed through Colton's mind as he managed to control bodily functions.

Then the critter continued to just wander on by, going northward or northeastward along the creek. They watched as the lumbering beast finally disappeared among the trees.

The encounter left both non-marmot hunters glad the event was over relatively quickly. There was no harm done. Now, though, they were wide awake, and Col, as usual in many situations, was sort of chatty. It was nervous chatter. Low tones and very quiet. Thankful chatter. Well, alright, Colton eventually brought Bill into the chatter, somewhat. Bill then had a story, remembering reading about wearing bells on your shoes to ward off bears or to at least let them know you were coming, as well as having pepper spray to kind of discourage them from getting too close. Bears must not want to be involved with humans any more than humans want to introduce themselves to bears was the general opinion discussed. Anyway, Bill also remembered reading about the difference between black bear scat and grizzly bear scat. Black bear scat contained berries and such, while grizzly scat had bells in it and smelled of pepper. While they had no bells, they were glad the bear appeared to be more interested in berries or something other than human flesh … or noodles or oatmeal.

And then, Bill admitted his earlier discovery. After a brief period of questioning – still in low tones – Colton was fine. After all, he had survived. And so had Bill.

Nervous, low laughter followed on and off as they talked themselves down from the excitement to eventually try to get some sleep. Col was probably the one who was nervous and laughing quietly. Who fell asleep first was uncertain, but apparently both did go to sleep. Finally. And after their bear encounter, the night was uneventful. There were no marmots … or killer goats.

The new morning came with some thankfulness for their survival, despite the fact that there are so few bear attacks during a typical year in the entire country. They were just glad that was not their time to be the statistics.

Three straight nights of varmints. Enough already! *Good grief.*

The poet Rumi visited again, through Bill, "'This being human is a guest house, every morning a new arrival…'"

"Glad I'm still around to welcome a new day," Colton noted. "Would still have my bells if I had any to begin with. But, for now, my mind is smelling bacon, but my nose oatmeal …"

Despite no bacon, the oatmeal was a winner, and a successful breakfast was partaken of.

"Had a friend, Bob, who lost his sense of taste and also his sense of smell." Colton started the next tale. "He told me that eventually the texture of food made the difference. He could remember the expected smell and imagine the expected taste of whatever he was eating. So, for me, this is bacon that has been mashed into some oatmeal-like concoction. I'll close my eyes and dream…"

Bill had learned in a few short days that sometimes you just listen to Colt. There was no need to respond or encourage him … just let him talk.

Their breakfast discussion evolved, though, and did include opinions on how to assess the life insurance risk of campers in any area considered "bear country". They agreed that they would not likely have any concern about considering that risk if anyone should volunteer their plans for such an adventure. The question would not typically arise about considering a person's risks to life and limb, at least based on what the men did for a living. No life insurance application either of them had ever seen asked a question like, "Do you plan within the next two years to hike and camp where bears frequent?" They actually weren't sure that question would even get approved by insurance departments as a legitimate question. Some people live near bears, but that had never come up in their underwriting experiences, either. Now, the question of mountain or rock climbing, along with other potentially hazardous avocations, had been seen in questions for life insurance applications.

The day ahead of them at that juncture was to head up toward Goat Lake and then try to find an accessible way to get over to Royal Basin. They were headed the same direction as their new friend – the non-man-eating, non-noodle-eating bear of the previous evening, but they were hoping a little (or a lot) that their black bear buddy had decided to head up into the trees. That said, they were fairly sure that men smelling of noodles (which would be them) would not necessarily draw a bear's attention. Of course, they also smelled of days without a change of clothes or a shower or any kind of bathing. The smell of noodles might be a plus for that bear.

Thankfully they had not brought beans.

The hike along the creek was uneventful. They were simply meandering along Home Creek. Bill referred to the area as Alder

Bottoms. The scent of the trees was different, and not easy for Col to describe years later. He also noted the light was odd. The trees seemed lighter on their trunks. They appeared to him to be more reflective.

They had passed the West Branch of Home Creek, and Bill's memory had been kicking in now and then, which he shared with Colt every so often. Maps seemed to be imprinted in his mind. Then came Heather Creek, a somewhat bigger merger of creeks that, with Home Creek, formed the Dungeness River. There weren't road signs to really help much, but with Bill's experiences in the area on numerous occasions and his decent memory of the maps he knew like the back of his ungloved hand, they did just fine. Bill could be instrumental in creating maps – if he wanted another career, Colt thought. And he might have had a map somewhere in the backpack, not that he needed guidance for this venture.

There was a clearing to the left at a turn in the river which appeared to be one of the options to head up towards the "pass with no name". They chose to continue to follow the river.

"Now, I'm thinking we need to name the pass, Bill," Colton proposed. "Actually, 'Pass with No Name' might work. Different than a horse with no name."

"For a second, I thought you wanted to name it 'Bill'. Well, maybe we could throw an idea out there to give that pass some name or other. That song you referenced describes somewhat of a trek, but we are not going to see a desert here."

Next, they came upon what could be Milk Creek. But again, there was no sign. There was another route desired, though.

There was this nice open area to their right – which should have been eastward. As they made their way toward the next entrant in the water flows of the area, the area opened up quite a bit more, with Ghoul Creek coming at them from kind of the east. That made them consider briefly whether or not there would be sightings of evil spirits or such in the area. At least their buddy, the bear, didn't appear to be haunted or possessed.

"This is the correct order of meeting up with this creek," Colton said. "Had we come upon this one before we last set up camp, well, that might have caused a little more angst for the visitor."

"That could be exactly why I didn't mention the creek – probably more because the name did not cross my mind, though, I also had no idea we would encounter a bear," came the response of Colton's guide and knowledge champion of the Olympic Trails.

Sidenote: Again, years later, Colton learned a lot more about what Bill knew and when he knew it.

Colton replied, "Not sure I believe in ghosts or ghouls or spirits … also not sure I want to validate their existence out here. Or anywhere really. Ignorance is bliss on that count."

Next up on the adventure of the day was Camp Handy. Now, they were back where they had spent their first night. Where they first had noodles. Where Colton had his first tent-building experience. It was a memorable spot, for sure – though, there was no plaque yet displayed. But there could be a sign saying, "DON'T BE LIKE COLTON!" in that very place someday, and that would bring them full circle, almost.

Trying to gain a perspective on where they had to go to meet up with Goat Lake, they realized they actually had to hike beyond the campsite just a little, something they had not considered, but it did not change their plan, at all.

They had not encountered the bear. Or his or her relatives. Or the other members of the sleuth. Or any evidence period of the bear. Life was indeed good. And they hadn't seen or heard any spirits, either. And Pinky wasn't to be found or her mom.

After finding the preferred route up to the lake – there seemed to be two, but the first looked a little more traveled, suggesting it made the better preference – they started up the mountain. The walk to the second possible route and back wasn't that far, about 600 feet, if that. They were at about 3,100 feet or so, at the riverside, heading toward a little over 5,900 feet above sea level.

They were going up, again.

Chapter Twenty-One

Making a Pass

The route was pretty narrow at first, but it opened up some as they made their way up. The path was extremely steep and slippery, not from ice or snow, but rather from loose rocks. It was a minimally maintained trail, at best. As they continued their ascent, the trees thinned out a little to their right, which the guys were fairly certain was north or northeast.

"This leafy vegetation is salal," Bill offered, continuing his nature lessons. "You can actually get a permit to harvest this. I never have. Not sure anyone would harvest along this way trail. I'm thinking elsewhere around here would be easier and more plentiful."

They were about a mile into the trek when the steepness significantly increased. Loose rocks were all over the place. The path taken, if it could be called a path, was precipitous. The stones made the trail extremely difficult to manage, making it feel at times to Colt that he was walking in place. That is, the stones kept shifting, so that pretty much every step seemed create the potential to slide backwards.

"What's with all these loose rocks? Good grief!" Colton exclaimed.

"Well, Charlie, it's called scree. It isn't fun climbing."

"Charlie?" Colton asked. "Oh, got it – 'Good grief'. Charlie Brown. I feel more like Michael Jackson doing some version of the moon walk. I was never able to do that, by the way."

"Nice dance move, but yeah, quite possibly not your thing, Col," Bill replied.

"Can't dance. Can't swim. Is an effort just walking sometimes ... or hiking," Colt added.

Struggling, they finally moved enough of the scree to form some footing. That, or they were just lucky and made some headway. The path widened as the trail snaked up the incline toward the lake. But they met their objective! It seemed really small, though, and there was no marker.

"No, this little water hole is not Goat Lake," Bill stated. "This is way too small."

Evidently, Colt was prematurely excited about nothing more than a puddle. He got over it. And they proceeded on. Around 500 feet or so farther, over a small incline, they finally got a view of the big lake – the real Goat Lake.

What a wonderful view!

It was the highest mountain lake they had encountered so far, and according to Bill, none coming up on the remainder of their hike would be that high above sea level. They could cook a whole lot of noodles with water through the pump from there.

The lay of the land beyond the lake didn't look too bad. There were peaks in a ridge, but not a whole lot higher than where they were then at the surface of the lake. There was also no snow or ice. Looked like more of that broken rock, though, but somewhat better, as there wasn't as much scree.

After a decent viewing of the lake and its surroundings, they trudged on. No pictures were taken.

Selecting what appeared to be a reasonable path up to what looked like a crest or ridge, the climb was trickier than they expected upon seeing it at lake level, but it didn't turn out to be horribly complicated. Could have been worse.

They arrived at the crest. A line from *Star Wars* came to Col's mind. *"It's worse."* Yes, it could be worse.

They were looking down on what Colton thought must be Royal Basin, but they had a trek ahead that looked like, oh, 1,500 feet or so down. It was hard to tell exactly, and the last several days had still not made him an expert on distances. The decline wasn't straight down, but it was much more of a "gradual angle" than what they had just came from to get to the lake and beyond. There were also more loose stones ahead, and more broken rocks. *Exhilarating. Exciting.*

I can go down backwards, Colton thought. But that wasn't such a great idea; however, it was another very Colton-esque idea. He had more of those ideas, too, all his very own – possibly as many as Bill had Rumi quotes. Bill had, of course, warned Colton, as we have noted, that most of his accidents over the years were on the way down versus while ascending. So, care was required.

Being as Colton had already experienced taking the fast lane down, he could lead. This time, the path was free of snow, but it still contained quite an incline with all the sliding potential of the loose stones. There were some trees to slow his descent, but he'd learned they weren't a perfect remedy for slowing down. He'd been there. Done that. The objective now was to get down the mountain versus across it. Adding to their difficulty were huge boulders – lots of them – in addition to a bunch of trees. One wrong slip and …

The primary route they were considering seemed to be mostly loose rocks. That said, all the routes were loose rocks. Fine rocks with the occasional mammoth boulder from car size to human size. Both were large enough to try avoiding in a slide, especially after picking up speed. Despite the threats here and there, the best idea seemed to be to follow the tricky crest a little farther south to find a less steep point with somewhat better footing opportunities to start down. The two thought that if one of them started sliding down, they would just make the best of it from wherever they stopped sliding versus spending any more time assessing the best possible route. They definitely didn't want to go back up to find a better way back down.

Sounds like a plan. May be edgy, but it was a plan, nonetheless.

The word "plan" reminded Colton of Ed, another of the people he had worked with over his forty-plus years in the risk assessment industry. Ed always greeted you with, "the man with a plan" or something like that. Obviously, Ed would not have been referring to them at that moment. What they had was more like a list of possibilities.

Thinking of Ed and another of his comrades from prior jobs, Ron, made Col think of the company coffee machine where they all worked. Why? Because Colton had not had his coffee for several days. Anyway, there was always a line at the machine just before 10:00 a.m. because that's when the free coffee stopped. There was no dollar slot back then either, only coins were accepted. It's really amazing what crosses your mind as you sense your life flashing before you, or you anticipate such a flash approaching. The lack of coffee had not caused issues for Colton till then. And he had never been one of those who absolutely required coffee before functioning or being spoken to in the morning. At the time of this Washington hiking adventure, he had been regularly having coffee for about five years. So, he was a "newbie" to the juice.

But back to their adventure down the mountain. Were there any falls or slips? No! Well, to hear Colton tell it, there were constant slippages. Generally speaking, though, it was a controlled journey of small bursts and steps, with momentary breaks for storytelling.

They made their way across the ridge. Neither fell, despite plenty of opportunities.

The road taken, perhaps by few, left them beyond the lake to the north. They then needed to employ backtracking to Royal Lake, following the creek, which was to their left, after they figured out where they were. Life is great when a plan falls together – not literally falls, but when it works out. You know what they're getting at here.

Night Six was approaching as they neared Royal Lake. The wear and tear of six days was having some impact on their motivation to carry on, as well as their physical capability of doing so. While the day's journey may not have been terribly far, the treacherous nature of the climb to Goat Lake and then to the crest and finally down the slope made their hike slow going at times. In a word, it was intense. A "grunt."

The city boy was learning a lot, but he was still inexperienced when it came to a lot of the details. And he was sore. Oh, he didn't complain a lot about that because he was too busy absorbing the world around him. There were, of course, pauses for his stories. The stories seemed to be told during those pauses the old man needed to gather himself along the way. "Gather himself" was a fitting synonym for "resting". He could stop, concentrate on the story he was telling, while resting, then he could proceed. That all worked – for him. And most of the time, Bill had no real complaint about story time or the stories themselves. There was a little charm in some of them. A little. Now, it was possible that Bill, too, appreciated a moment to rest, although Col gave him the benefit of the doubt that with his experience hiking, he may not have absolutely required said breaks – at least as often as Col needed them.

"Are there any caves around this area?" Colt asked for who knows what reason.

"There are some on the park property, a lot closer to the ocean. Not any big ones near here that I immediately recall. Have you been in caves?"

"Some."

And that led to essentially a "Colton Life Story" about his cave experiences (Note: You can enjoy that story earlier in this book – don't want to repeat it here.)

Royal Lake was quiet. The marmots weren't making a lot of racket, whistling at each other or at the guys, but they were there. No other humans were there, though. And there was no evidence they had been there, either. No trash. No tents. Nothing.

They had their choice of where to set up their tents, and so, they took a very short amount of time to explore the options before settling on what Colt called "a nice area" near the lake.

The menu called for noodles for their sixth dinner ... again. And that would be without the addition of chicken or marmot. Speaking of which, they hadn't seen chickens at all – they weren't in Key West – but there were marmots all over the place, as you know. They were presumably around Goat Lake, too, but they did not notice them. Course, they weren't paying attention or listening for them as they had their focus elsewhere, such as being too busy sliding around on the scree. The critters lived on to whistle another day.

No bears were around that night – that they saw. No evidence was seen of them, either. The one from the creek camp site could still be on their tail.

But … they enjoyed another dinner. There was more conversation. Despite knowing each other through business relationships for years, they were still learning much more about growing up, what led to their career choices, and numerous other fun facts of life. It was all good. They were both happy. And they were adding to their life stories with each new day. And this day had added a lot of "what happened" to their storylines, as they recalled the scree, the lake, the ridge, everything about what turned out to be quite an exacting trek from the Dungeness River. They had endured a tough day of hiking.

Tent life seemed grand that night. *Who needs a perfect sleeping mattress or a high level of any hotel accommodations?* They were too tired and sore and stiff to even feel like discussing the issue or all the possibilities.

Chapter Twenty-Two

Royal Treatment, with a Flair

Awakening near the lake was hours after retirement – that is, after they had retired to their tents. There had been no beasts in their camp. No encyclopedia or vacuum cleaner salespeople. No visitors of any kind. Just a calm, peaceful night. And after the night prior – actually, the three nights prior – that was very much welcomed. Life was good.

It was also good to be up and about "taking nourishment" (in the form of breakfast), as one of the doctors Col knew from his career used to say.

Colton noticed a gluten-free critter in the lake. *Was that a trout?* He wondered if he had actually seen any living creature on the trip. He guessed he probably had, just couldn't recall anything … oh, other than the bear. And marmots.

And then, the Colton storytelling began anew, spurred by who knows what.

"I remember when I was first married – really, the first time – that we had a cemetery salesperson call. Bill, I actually said, 'Sure, stop by – yes, tomorrow evening.' My new bride realized then that I needed to have reduced phone privileges. Anyway, the guy shows up. He was talking about plots – cemetery plots – and my new bride all of a sudden turned to me and, with a strained look and anxious voice, while cupping her face, says something like, 'Don't let them bury me! Bugs will get in! I can't stand the thought of bugs!' She was acting all irrational. 'I want my ashes spread over Central State Hospital!' That was the nearby mental hospital. The guy seemed to accelerate his presentation, gave us some reading material, and left. Then she turned to me and said, 'That worked.' Well, I never made another sales appointment that I recall."

"Did you buy?"

Colton confirmed that they had not and noted that the salesperson did not say much after the Central State Hospital remark. Col supposed he could have been concerned he was dealing with an escapee or one out on a temporary leave.

All was good until Col decided to sing …

Not that there was much to complain about (and definitely nothing Col should be singing about), as their dietary needs were being met (they did not go hungry), but breakfast at McDonald's might be welcomed at least once after returning to what many would call civilization.

Col sang the jingle from some time in the 70's that started out, "'Breakfast at McDonald's is served with a Flair...'" The old Flair pen. 'For writing while you're dining.'"

Bill didn't remember the little tune. But he likely got enough of it real fast, at least with Colton singing it.

So, let's see – he can't swim, can't dance, can't sing, can't walk on glaciers. There are many "can't's". Col is a "cantor" – almost, but ... no ...

At least Colton loved music, although he wasn't able to reproduce songs. There was a time that he could carry a tune, without the benefit of a bucket. That might have been before his thumb injury. The thumb injury could have quashed his musical nerve. Or was that a muscle? He might be onto something, though, as he did recall being able to sing before the pass that was launched at him that fateful evening.

Back to oatmeal time ...

There certainly had not been a lot of "planning" involved with their meals. There was no cookbook on a stump beside their fire. No myriad of spice containers. No mixing bowls. No aprons. But there were no complaints about any of that. Life was good. The decision was made over breakfast, after the music stopped, to wander around the basin, without musical accompaniment, and then head toward the Royal Creek campsite, which was approaching the Dungeness River. Awakening there the next morning should get them to their car sometime during the next day, likely early in the day, toward mid-day, after their seventh night in the wild.

The important consideration was that they were running low on noodles. They had one more dinner and that was all. Colton had already decided that there might be years before he tried noodles again. Not even with the addition of marmot, chicken, or bear.

Their next decision was to head basically south toward what might be the upper part of the basin, following Royal Creek toward the area between Mount Deception and Mount Fricaba. There was a rise above the lake to a large rock and then a trail through some forested area to another meadow. Bill called the area Arrowhead Meadow. There was a small, murky lake at the end of the trail and possibly the beginning of Royal Creek. Above them, on the side of Mount Deception, was what looked like a real glacier, as opposed to the one leading into Home Lake.

Looking up at Mount Deception and the surrounding ridges made Bill believe that they had made the correct decision to not go up into the Deception Basin. There was a huge amount of snow from the Royal Lake perspective. Bill could not pinpoint the Colton-esque routes (those that did not require any technical gear or training) from their vantage point, making him think that they were likely covered by snow. Regardless, they were not going to go back, even if the route appeared open – they didn't have enough noodles. Not enough oatmeal, either. And there was never enough bacon.

The air smelled fresh. The creek seemed to be formed from the runoff of the snow and snowfields, which made sense. The question in Col's mind of a possible spring source was more or less answered. They had actually seen what looked to be a spring, though, on the Constance Pass Trail below Sunnybrook Meadow toward the Dosewallips River.

Colton talked about his journey to a lake in the middle lower peninsula of Michigan, where there were several springs that seemed to help keep the lake filled. The lake was known to be spring fed, so again, that made sense. As the lake froze every winter, the last places to freeze were over the springs. Those areas stood out. They looked like dark, round circles on the forming ice. Walking on the ice was a pastime of the residents (and guests), but you stayed away from the spots where the springs were until everything was firmly frozen (meaning the dark circles disappeared). (Note: This is NOT an instructional manual on ice walking, as Col is no expert … on that either … though, he never fell through the ice.)

"I thought you didn't swim," Bill noted.

"No, I don't. But you can't swim when it's frozen, even if I could," came Col's false retort.

"It could break," Bill argued.

"Yes. Well, I suppose. Never experienced that. I do remember once a bunch of us – a dozen or so, as I recall – were standing around a hole in the ice cut to fish, watching the attempt of the youngster, my stepson, with the pole. All of a sudden, there was a very loud pop – ice popping. Loudest pop I ever recall hearing. Everyone scattered. What they say, whoever 'they' are, is that ice popping could be actually freezing, not necessarily cracking or thawing. Or at least changing with the temperature moving up or down and so forth."

"How thick was the ice?" Bill asked.

"Let's see. About fourteen inches thick, as I remember, and the water depth in the area where that hole was cut was no more than about fourteen feet in the middle of the channel. One of the neighbors had a large manual auger to cut the ice holes. That was about six inches across – not really sure."

"How deep did the lake get?"

Colton thought that it might have been 30-some feet, almost 40, at its deepest point, but he was, again, not sure. (We didn't "fact-check" that, either, but rather allowed his estimate to stand.)

"I guess a platform of ice fourteen inches thick over water about fourteen feet deep below that ice is kind of scary, if you think of the whole scenario that way and disregard science – not that any science I knew reassured me," Colton offered. "But I walked on it. What I never saw was the ice just slipping away. The way they described that was the ice was there and then the ice just kind of sinks, almost all at once, and it's gone until the next year."

Colton went on to explain that he loved being on the water, any water, in a boat or kayak, with a life jacket, or even being pulled on a tube, again with a life jacket, despite not having any idea how to swim. He still wasn't sure he could get over his fear to learn to swim. Seemed a little strange with his fondness for the water, but entirely possible. Colton did remember once getting dumped off a tube in deep lake water. He couldn't remember how deep – about 25 or so was his guess. He just bobbed in the water, he said, awaiting to be rescued. He wasn't sure, but he thought that was about the same place on the lake where he took off and dumped his last wife off a boat. Colton said he had been perplexed all that afternoon on how he could have accelerated so fast as to throw her out of the boat or, as she put it, "tried to kill her". Then, he said that she casually said, in describing the event later to others at the lake, that she was on the back swim platform of the boat, not IN the boat. (As your narrator, I'm thinking this was yet another example of Colt's inability to be a marriage counselor as an alternative career … it would not look good on his resume to say, "accused of trying to kill ex-spouse", whether true or not.)

Colton had yet another story about that same lake …

Years ago, the person who may have owned the lake (this specific detail was not available to Colt, at that moment) or the largest part of the property (or a vacation retreat on the shore), decided to dig two channels that would become connections between that lake and the next lake north. Seemed like a great idea. People could navigate between the two lakes. The owner was about halfway to the next lake, perhaps even a little closer, when someone decided to check the elevation of the two lakes. The channels would have pretty much emptied the lake north. So, yeah, it turned out not to be a great idea. On the bright side, the misadventure allowed more homes to have a dock on the channel extensions, with access to the lake. At least some thought that was a good thing – likely the channel dwellers.

"That was and is a wonderful place to visit. Great people. The guy with the auger and his wife let us stay with them several times. That led to a great game of trading jokes on each other. The first time I stayed there, I noted down on the porch by the lake that the lady of the house had a collection of Coke birdhouses. So, the next time I stayed there, I brought an IU birdhouse – same colors. And I went down and replaced one of hers with mine. Her husband caught me, but just smiled. Didn't say a word. That was in September, as I recall. She didn't notice the IU one until spring. They were MSU Spartan fans, so the game was on. The next spring, we had green light bulbs on the porch, and then green tulips came up. Yes – green tulip flowers. Really strange. So, my wife and I – this is the same spouse I tried to kill …"

"You admit it!" Bill shouted.

"No, no – that was only for identification purposes for the story I was telling you. Anyway, the two lake dwellers went somewhere for several days. We planted bulbs – those flowers that even pop out of snow at times. Crocuses. We planted them in the shape of the IU logo – the I through the U. In the middle of their yard. No harm. Even if you mow them down, they come up the next year … a gift that keeps on giving. The day before they were taking off for a spring venture, they noticed the arrangement. Enough popped up that they could see the logo. My best work!"

Story time over, and after wandering up toward the beginnings of Royal Creek and the surrounding area, observing many marmots they could have bagged, Colt and Bill headed out past Royal Lake, following the trail. Sometimes, that meant they were near the creek, and sometimes, they were a little bit away. Marmots were around. But no marmots were harmed in the completion of the hiking/camping adventure. Suddenly, there was some sort of bird – Bill called them grouse. Colton thought he said "gross" at first, then he made the distinction.

"I'm surprised we haven't seen more of them," Bill noted. "They are usually all over the place."

Tiredness was creeping in somewhat, even though the time was not even noon – or what they thought should be noon. They really had no idea what time of day was upon them. There were moments in the previous several days when they grew tired, but something always happened to elevate their game. The presence of a bear would do that, for example. The fact that they still had a long way to go to get back to the car might also do the trick. So far that day by Royal Lake, there was nothing happening to provide any elevating of their energy, aside from the beauty around them. The closest big moment to that point in their day had been identifying a cloud that appeared to be shaped like a goat. It was the little things that were then being embraced – the clouds, the trees, the mountains … perhaps not so little things, but you see what we're after here.

"Did Rumi have any mountain quotes?" Col asked.

"Yes. Several. There was one about your words echoing back to you, as I recall," Bill said, but he had no others handy, at that moment.

(If Bill was unable to recall more Rumi on request, he was likely as tired as the city boy, but I digress …)

In discussing the goat cloud, they realized that one creature they had not encountered was a mountain lion (or cougar or puma or the big cat known by any number of names depending on where you lived). The reason that thought came up was that there were tracks hardened in some mud near a stream. And they very well may have been mountain lion tracks. Mercury Cougar was easier to say, they surmised, and easier to sell than a Mercury Mountain Lion. That led to a discussion about other car names and their origins. Like Pacer. Colton thought the Indiana Pacers front office might be glad that Pacer cars were no longer built, versus being tempted to award their top player any given year with one of those. You could hear a player possibly saying, "Please release me – let me go…" (And no, Colt didn't attempt to sing that). That said, some players may have liked the car well enough to buy one.

Then there was the Edsel. Named after a Ford family member, at least that's what Colton thought. *Was that vehicle built for about three seasons or years?* One of Colt's brothers had three or four of them – he thought one from each year.

The Yugo. Neither owned one and neither recalled knowing anyone who had one. That one received some bad press back in the day. Easy to pick up and move or so "they" said. If the car quit running, a small number of people could carry the poor thing to the side of the road out of traffic.

When Colton was a kid, about nine or ten years old, he recalled his stepfather having a Hudson. That might have been a 1950 model year car – he couldn't remember exactly. It wasn't fancy, but that car was reliable. His stepdad might have traded the first one in on another one.

There were also cars "first on race day" or "fix or repair daily", depending on your preference in vehicles.

Alas, no cars appeared in the clouds. Just the goat if, but, for a short moment. No boats appeared, either. No Flair.

As they progressed toward the Dungeness River, there were the usual large boulders now and then. There was the sound of water all around. Waterfalls, occasionally, several creeks, and some rivulets. Those seemed to be a mainstay of the Olympic Area. They were growing a little too tired to enjoy them nearly as much as they might have earlier in their adventure. Waterfalls are always cool, though – even small ones. There were also rapids pretty much most of the way, bringing a refreshing and relaxing sound. Soothing. And that made rest sound even better.

Everett Kunzelman

Chapter Twenty-Three

Miracle Along Royal Creek

Every so often, as the two guys made their way onward, there were more open areas around Royal Creek. They had passed Mount Walkinshaw, which they had to look back at to get a good view, and there was a wide opening heading up toward the summit just murmuring to them, "Come climb me." But that wasn't in their cards that day. Although, it looked more possible to conquer than the scree below Goat Lake. The mountain used to be named The Citadel, but it was renamed in the 1960's for a gentleman named Walkinshaw, who was instrumental in the conservation efforts to create Olympic National Park – a little history lesson for the walk, brought to them by Bill. The peak stood out, being almost 7,400 feet above sea level and approaching, oh, 3,000 feet above the creek. (Most everything was close to 3,000 feet up from wherever they were out there in the Olympics … or so it seemed.)

At the base of this clearing near the creek, they encountered a large number of fallen trees, which made passage a smidge more interesting. After navigating the downed trees, they were in a nice valley carved by the creek over a long time. *Isn't that how ravines, valleys, and canyons are made? Over some period of time … by water? Possibly.* This was a different type of beauty from what they had experienced so far on their journey, and that reminded Colton somewhat of the Big Thompson River Canyon in Colorado, leading into Estes Park. There were no warning signs there along Royal Creek to climb to safety in the event of a flash flood, but it appeared to be somewhat easier to climb along Royal Creek than along certain sections of the Big Thompson, where the rock walls were quite steep and without many places to grab onto by a climbing rookie. There were still rocks to navigate by the creek, but they appeared less threatening. Far less likely as well was a flash flood occurring on Royal Creek. Why? A snowfield wasn't going to melt that quickly so as to cause a flash flood. A "broken" spring would not do the trick, either. Could have a "cloud burst", though, that would create a lot of water all at once.

While approaching the last campsite for their seven-day ordeal, there were humans. And, again, a mix of males and females, this group heading the opposite direction, toward Royal Lake. The guys were just going to wave, speak politely, and keep going, but this group was more talkative. There was plenty of time prior to "lights out" (as Colton referred to bedtime or sleeping bag time), so that was fine. Colton was somewhat hesitant to use his real name, but he did anyway. As luck would have it, there was no reference made to the Mount Rainier public service posters of yesteryear.

From what Colton recalled, there were two of the new humans who were related – a brother and sister – and the other three were friends of the two. They had parked where Bill had parked at the Upper Dungeness Trailhead and had ventured in from there, sometime late that morning. The siblings were from Boise (or that area of Idaho). The friends were from the Seattle area. The siblings were on a mission, so to speak, to spread their grandfather's ashes at Royal Lake, a place that he had held dear. Their grandmother's ashes had been spread there by their grandpa about ten to fifteen years earlier. *What a mission.* The friends were assisting in getting the siblings to the lake, where they thought they might spend one or two nights and then hike around the general area for a couple more days or so. Despite the serious nature of their trek, they appeared to be having fun while doing what grandpa wanted done. Grandpa likely would have wanted them to have fun, too.

Turned out, one of the three friends accompanying the brother and sister lived just a mile from Bill. But they had never met that either recalled, although both loved the Elysian Brewery on Pike that was near where they lived – walkable by each. Colton at least could add a word or two, as he knew of Elysian. Somewhere back home, he had seen the beer. So, that made him feel a part of the overall conversation The other two Seattle friends of the siblings lived in the Beacon Hill area of the city, and they said there was an Elysian Brewery taproom not too far from their homes as well.

Small world moment. And all survived the moment. Their hikes in opposite directions continued.

Neither Bill nor Colton had ever spread anyone's ashes anywhere. They did not really get into a discussion with the siblings on why grandpa spread grandma's ashes at Royal Lake (another weak interviewing moment for Colton). And neither of our boys had given much thought to where their ashes might be spread, if they were to be spread, at all. Bill thought somewhere in the mountains would be great, but he would have to think about which mountains. Colton had no idea, wondering if maybe Shades State Park could be the spot for him. Or perhaps it would be some other forested area. Colton thought there was always a chance that he would live in the woods someday, and that another place might pop up as a possibility. He did not seem to think burial was all that attractive, but he realized that, when the time came, he likely would not be in a position to argue.

"You would think spreading ashes might reduce the significance of bug issues, though," Bill suggested.

Col agreed, reminding his friend that the "bug complaint" was part of the "Can we get this salesperson out of our house?" gambit.

"Do you think those humans became aware, as we all stood around, that we have not bathed for days?" Colton asked.

Bill shook his head as they continued the hike and said, "I think we were far enough apart that running into the guy at Elysian won't be an issue. I will say this, though … after many camping or hiking or climbing expeditions, on our way out of the woods, as we passed by people, I tended to smell soap or shampoo scents. Maybe even perfume. Makes me wonder if the other noses were as sharp as mine, perhaps to their dismay."

Colton then told the story of the Appalachian Trail hiker that his daughter and he had met. Colt could not recall smelling anything, but, then he admitted that, sometimes, his nose fails him.

Finally, they made their way to their last night's camping site.

The Royal Creek Campsite was kind of below a ridge named Gray Wolf (the American spelling of "gray"). Baldy was a little farther down the ridgeline – a peak with one simple name – no "mount" before the name or "peak" added, just Baldy. There need to be more prominent mountains with one simple name, don't you think? Like the well-known Everest and Rainier.

Now then, about the issues of "gray" versus "grey" …

Grateful Dead used the "e" spelling in "Touch of Grey". Colton commented on that and thought that might have been the Dead's only Top 40 hit. Could be true. Without the internet where they were, the situation was like the old days – they didn't know the answer, for sure. Later, they would look it up … if they remembered to. Neither of them, despite their ages, could remember life prior to having the world of knowledge right at their fingertips, but both had been in the world without that benefit – Colton, the elder, more so than Bill, the youngster. That was just the way things were anymore, though, but their hiking and camping exploit had suddenly brought back the time of discussing things with no confirmed answer available.

While they probably could have arrived at the trailhead where the car was parked that evening versus camping one more night, this was an opportunity for one last supper of noodles. They did not want to miss that. No. The last supper of the trek. No marmot, bear, goat, or chicken enhancement protein to be added. Just noodles. One more time. There was a chance that they just wanted to complain one more time about the noodles. Or Colton did, anyhow. Bill was the chef. He ate his own cooking … very chef-like, wasn't it? There was also one last breakfast – Colt's mind-smelled bacon, which, in reality, was oatmeal.

Another reason for not rushing back to the car was that the day had already seemed relatively long. And Bill thought the trail from the murky lake to Dungeness might be close to seven miles long. They had tracked part of that twice, but they would have to hang on for a few more miles. Tiredness was settling in relatively fast, as the wear and tear of the previous several days came crashing down upon them. Or at least it did for Col.

For a first ever camping experience, Col had quite the encounter to recall, lie about, and tell some half truths about – all of that. But it wouldn't be tonight. Their tents popped open just as they had for the prior six nights. Without any mechanical issues. It had been a perfect week of tent building.

And a campfire! They made a campfire – a first on their venture! They were in an area where they could have a fire and, so, why not? Bill explained the rules, but Col forgot them until later – they had something to do with the elevation and the specific area, like not inside a national park. There were plenty of small limbs, so they weren't going to have a bonfire, but they got the thing going without too much trouble. The smaller the fire, the less embers they'd have to snuff out.

Noodles were eaten around the fire. That did not enhance their flavor, but it may have been better than served with marmot. Highlights of the week were reviewed … some, not a lot. Possible exaggerations were discussed that they could tell friends, and the details of the big stories were coordinated between the two of them (only to be forgotten, perhaps by morning – if even remembered that long). For example, Colt's fall was lengthened and then shortened again; however, they decided the landing, as described earlier and apparently accurately, was likely as good as the story could possibly get. Colton offered to sing the entire jingle about the Flair pen because they had time to spare, but that offer was rejected. There would be no more singing.

Colton's left knee was feeling decent. All was well. His thumb was also okay for the moment.

And then Bill pulled out more wine …

"Jesus?" Colton asked.

"No, no … the water was not turned into wine. Just happened to have another half bottle safely secured, hidden," answered their temporary savior.

Thankfully, the bear the other evening didn't have a nose for wine.

All in all, it seemed like the perfect ending to this last supper on their expedition, even if categorized as "rotgut" by the hiking leader.

"Having wine in a tin cup made me think we should have had oysters and beer earlier," Colt noted.

"There must be a story?" a semi-intrigued Bill asked.

"No, not this time," Colt said. "You quote Rumi, I sometimes quote Buffett, or at least reference words in one of his songs. 'Tin Cup Chalice' is the song, in this case."

"Cannot recall Rumi mentioning tin cups, oysters, or beer. He does frequently mention wine, though."

"Sad, no tin cup reference," Colton said.

Their campsite was thought by far to be the darkest of the seven nights, but then the site where they encountered Yogi might have been somewhat darker. They had indeed had some great settings for campsites. Each one, in its own respect, was special, with some unique attribute to make it memorable. Even Colton might be able to remember a lot of the story about each of the nights, without a ton of notes. Well, maybe. And that last night with a fire made the place better than the evening could have been otherwise. So, yeah, much more memorable.

Colton reached for his pad and pen to record some last thoughts. But he could not immediately find the notepad. He may have to rely on whatever memory was still available to him while approaching age 60. He would have to sleep on that thought.

Sleep felt good. But it didn't help his memory …

Chapter Twenty-Four

To the Trailhead and Beyond

Another day dawned and still without any rain. No one was going to believe that.

Breakfast was upon them. Oatmeal was eaten ... again. Colton had a smile on his face. Oatmeal was all good. He was concerned, though, that his visualization of bacon while eating oatmeal could be an issue down the road. His taste buds being inadequate at times anyway made him decide to focus his mind on the oats. There was a little brown sugar taste manufactured as well. Maple, too.

He realized then that he had survived the mind game about bacon, and he noted he had indeed survived all the mental aspects of everything else about the hiking adventure. What he should have done was use the game on noodles.

Despite having a "goal" only to get back to the car that day, they still had to packed up, as they had done every other day. There would be no dragging stuff behind them on the trail. No. No dumping. Absolutely not.

The time had arrived. The week was over, as difficult as it was to believe. Col thought they could make a career of this camping thing, but then he remembered … noodles. Seven nights was enough of noodles. At least for the time being. When noodles changed, then there could be some discussion. Or perhaps when dehydrated marmots were a thing.

Leaving camp was enhanced by Bill remembering the Flair song but not mentioning it. That, to him, at least Colton's rendition, might have been worse than seven days of noodles. They each had special memories and moments to savor. Or maybe savor wasn't the right word, but whatever.

And here was an interesting fact: they had no noodles to pack and no oatmeal to pack. Both were gone. How was that for perfect food planning?

They headed back toward the car. The distance from the Royal Creek Camp to the Upper Dungeness Trailhead was about the same as they had covered the first day from the Trailhead to Camp Handy, and today, they had a much earlier start. The first few miles (maybe it was yards that seemed like miles?) down the creek to the Dungeness River were all new. They had not been on this trail in its entirety on the first day, as they had followed the Dungeness River. Of course, Colton was confused as to where they were.

There were more rapids. The trail down toward the river was more of a decline or downward pitch than expected – not the smooth, flat exit Colt thought it would be. It seemed as if the trail would know he was tired by now and offer him something easier as a way out. But no. There was another trail off to the left that Col thought might be one of the lesser maintained ones – the way trails. At the river again, going the opposite way on the same trail was again something new. There was lots of moss. And the amazing light they had seen the first day was back. *The sun pierced the trees, brightening up all the woods – the trees, the undergrowth, the trail. It was very welcoming. Very vivid.* The old growth forest was all around them, *once again.*

They weren't sure of the total miles covered from the Royal Camp, but they made reasonably good time. The bridge across the Dungeness was still in place. Colton loved that bridge. But they did not run into any people. Pinky was gone – she might have been the other direction, though … had to be, Col thought. And he hoped her mom had gotten her rest and her dad had survived the experience as a single parent in the mountains.

Arriving at the trailhead, they were happy to see their car was still there. There was no thought that it wouldn't have been, but there was a degree of excitement to just sit on a comfortable seat for a little bit even if it wasn't a favorite chair back home. At least it wasn't a Yugo, a boulder, or a stump. So, there they sat. For a few minutes, they simply accepted the reality of their week in the wilderness before contemplating the ride back to Bill's place.

The man with wine reached back to a container in the back of the car which held ceremonial warm beer and salty snacks – chips, this time. A tradition like no other, Bill explained, the master guide was to offer up one last memory for the newcomer at the end of a camping expedition, at least that's what Bill's climbers were used to at the end of their many journeys.

The plan for the drive back would be to avoid as many humans as possible by making no stops – they would even stay in the car on the ferry for that very purpose. Remember, they had been seven days and nights in the same clothes. Colton also had forgotten to "change" his underwear – as in forwards, backwards, inside, outside. So, there was no plan to stop anywhere. Just get back to Bill's place, shower (or hose off outside), burn (or at least tightly bag) the clothes, and then go out to eat.

"I know this great noodle place…," Bill announced, letting the thought trail off as Colton just kind of sat there, his head dropping for just a moment.

"But do they have marmot on the menu?"

Bill did not think so.

Maybe chicken.

They then agreed that it would be a place without noodles or oatmeal. Tomorrow morning? Maybe oatmeal for Colton, but he was very excited that he could also have bacon!

And so, the drive back to civilization, as they knew life, commenced. Col was surprised that, after not driving for a week,

Bill didn't need lessons. It was kind of like riding a bicycle. Bill noted that, after days of traveling at walking speed, even twenty miles an hour seemed awfully fast, at first. Being as they were on a dirt road initially, where getting to sixty wasn't likely, they could slowly adjust to higher speeds. Cell service jumped in somewhere on the way to the main roads. But they really had adjusted to being without it and were not really looking for a connection to the world.

Colton's phone finally "beeped" or something, and he immediately searched "marmot", discovering that some think they taste like wild duck, some think they're kind of beefy. Those who had tried the rodent, or if you prefer, ground squirrel, just weren't sure. Not "ground" as in prepared through grinding, but "ground" as in living on or in or near the ground. (The grinding terminology reminding them of an old *SNL* "ad" – the Bassomatic. "That's good bass!" Marmot would not have had the same ring for the line, at all.) Regardless, all Col cared about really was that there would be no noodle dish of any kind in his near future.

He also discovered that, yes, you need a hunting license to hunt marmots. Good thing the guys were law-abiding fellas. What a rap sheet that could have been: they had bagged marmots without a license.

On the way back, Bill mentioned his amazement at how many trees in the area had been cut, almost clear cut, noting it had been done most of the time closer to the highways. He wondered about forest management and how that kind of thing operated. For the most part, there hadn't been places they saw while hiking and camping that appeared to have been cut for many years, if at all. There had been a lot of good-sized trees everywhere.

Colton thought he had heard that industrial owners of forests do clear cutting and replanting on some schedule, while property owned by the federal government or conservancy groups do more precise cutting to accomplish a mixed growth including older and newer trees. Col didn't know the specifics of the Washington Department of Natural Resources.

The bridges had survived the week, including the floating one, which came along first. No storms had knocked it out. The sun, which had been plentiful, didn't melt the bridge, either. Things were moving along well.

Then, right there on the 305, were the Golden Arches! Colton, being semi-oblivious to their surroundings, did not see them. But Bill did, Colton later learned. Apparently, he had a momentary fear of the old man breaking into song. The old man did not, however, and the arches were soon behind them, and all was well again.

The ferry also lived on to serve as their way to follow 305 across the water. And it was better than swimming, for those who knew how to swim, that is. Then, Seattle traffic was upon them, and it had not changed much, if at all, in a week. There were no obvious traces of recent rain in town – so what was the thing about it being the rainy city? At least there was no obvious evidence of rain, such as huge puddles or flash floods.

And then, they were at the apartment – Bill's bachelor pad … two bedrooms, plastered walls, molded additions to the ceilings, and hardwood floors.

This was built in the '30's. Neat old building," Bill said. "Being on the top floor looking westerly … there are great sunsets in my living room!"

His view included the Seattle downtown, Puget Sound, and even Mount Constance and the Olympic Mountains. Bill described the sky as "Wagnerian". That description, along with quoting Rumi, made Colt believe there was a lot more to his friend culturally than using a tin cup as a chalice, which seemed to be Colt's culture.

There was a shower in Bill's apartment – thankfully. And hot water. Somehow, the world was becoming right again. He had trash bags to tie off with the week's garb securely inside. Colt sure hoped the bag didn't get opened by airport security. Maybe he should stuff some of his leftover, unsullied toilet paper in there.

Dinner was a walkable distance from Bill's apartment, so why not take advantage of that? They had been walking – no, HIKING – for days, so there had been a lot of practice for a walk to dinner. They might miss the Wagnerian sunset from his apartment, but they would always have that sunset and moon rise on Del Monte Ridge.

The restaurant was near Twelfth and Pike. Barrio served Mexican food, actually it primarily served Mexican (And they had margaritas!).

When you had lived someplace forever, the local establishments get to know you. That was true there for Bill. He was identifiable, even after seven days wandering the Olympic woods. The bartender/waiter knew Bill by name (and vice versa

– Colt was introduced, but he could not remember their names). That meant, they should get reasonably good service … as opposed to a certain restaurant in Chicago where they purposefully treat you obnoxiously. The fact that Bill had always been a good customer was a plus as well at Barrio. He had always behaved there, he claimed.

The menu had no marmot delicacy. They were disappointed. The waiter said that they did not usually acquire "meat" from local "hunters". *Good idea.* There likely are restaurants that did (and do) – not going to surmise where or what "meat" is offered at those establishments or where said restaurants might be located. The non-marmot offerings were considered, and selections made. Dinners other than noodles were ordered. There were enough tequilas to keep one busy sampling for, well, days – let's just say it should take days versus one evening.

All seemed right with the world again.

PART III

DRAWING CONCLUSIONS

(Colton's Life After the Big Event)

Chapter Twenty-Five

Adjusting to the Original (Non-noodle) Life

Dinner was exceptional. Gluten-free. But not a noodle to be found. And there was no singing – the restaurant didn't have the big Sombrero, celebratory singing that some "Mexican" restaurants do. Everyone was happy. The lack of singing was definitely a cause of the contentment.

Colton was not sure his stomach would be amenable to non-noodles after his seven-day ordeal … nor to the gluten. But he took the chances.

"When did the gluten issue develop – or was that condition always there?" Colton asked.

Bill thought for a second and answered, "Let's see. That started in the late '80's. I was in Mexico, southern Mexico, and Guatemala."

"And we're eating Mexican food?" the super observant Colton announced.

"Yes, but there are options. Anyway, I was gluten-free before gluten-free was cool. Could be a song. Don't sing."

"I'm not that fast or creative," Colton assured his friend.

"My system has not been the same since. One of those things," Bill said and sighed.

Their conversation was nothing like some of the conversations among underwriters at a typical lunch in a company cafeteria. Thinking of the conversations at his places of work, Colton figured if those were the topics they were discussing now, some nearby people would get up and move. Their case discussions at lunch were a little over the top for a lunch, or any meal. They weren't meant to be purposefully disruptive. They were just an extension of their workday conversations. Discussing the issues sort of helped release some of the pain you felt for others' misfortunes. The argument could be made that there was some stress associated with reading horrible medical histories, especially if the proposed insured was a child.

"Ever have one of those lunch discussions where non-underwriters would get up and move?" Colton asked.

Bill said that he had not and wasn't aware of any where people were actually upset enough to move.

"The ones about gastrointestinal ailments would have been the worst," Colt continued. "Kind of like this one with more feeling and detail, maybe. Or some other unusual disorder … anything that kind of made you feel uncomfortable. And the really ugly stuff. Discussing the matter seemed to have made you feel better after you'd reviewed a file, but not so necessarily for everyone within earshot."

They both agreed that they never purposefully had a disgusting lunch table discussion just to have one, but sometimes, case discussions just happened from their morning's work. The extension of their work. They really should have been more aware of their surroundings back then, but they were much younger. Kids really. Now? They were more in control. Subtle. Quiet. Using more TLAs worked better.

"Likely don't want to have actuaries at the table. They get a bad rap sometimes," Colton surmised. "Although, I like some of the jokes. Of course, many of the jokes could be targeted at any group. The best one or, okay, the ONLY one I can remember – can't remember most jokes – is something about the extroverted actuary who looks at your shoes when talking to you whereas the introverted looks at their own shoes. Or something like that. There are probably underwriters like that. Or others."

And then Colton remembered one of his first evening dinners with reinsurance people – the company was a Midwestern company. Reinsurance providers cover excess loss on policies for a fee – insurance on insurance, sort of. The group had gone out for pizza in Broad Ripple – an Indianapolis neighborhood with shops, bars, and eateries – and were then going to a Pacer game (There was no car award ceremony at half-time that Col recalled). Col thought one of his friends he still sees who lives near Indy, named Bob, was in the group. Bob might deny that, he said. Col couldn't remember much except the pizza, and he didn't know who won the game, but at a restroom break, one of the other guys from the reinsurance company belts out in the restroom that his urine tested "two plus for pepperoni". Underwriters will get that – and medical people. To his knowledge, Colton knew of no "pepperoni test" for urine analysis or urinalysis.

The conversation then moved to their big experience out in the Olympics. There was no discussion or attempt to rate the "best meal". That category was completely set aside. I mean, they had no pizza … no bacon. Now Colton did like the oatmeal, and he mentioned that. So, their urine would have tested positive for noodles as well as oatmeal … and that's it.

The best campsite? They both agreed that the ridge, Del Monte Ridge, watching the moon rise and sunset was the winner. No question, at all. The silver went to … well, there were two that got votes, so there was a tie. Camp Handy was Colton's choice and that might have been driven in part by his very first night camping ever, but also the sound of the water had won him over. Bill kind of liked Home Lake or Royal Lake – a lake guy, quite possibly. He was split on which was the absolute best – or second best. Colton liked those two as well, but then they discussed the meadow. He had almost forgotten the quiet there, except for the grazing mountain goat. Picking the last place finisher was rough. All were good. Probably the "bear lodging" was seventh. Both seemed to agree on that, but they noted that was their very own creation, as it wasn't a formal campsite. So, their own creation was last, and that's why they weren't camping planners for a living … not that Bill couldn't be one.

The best view? There were several candidates again – not that Colton would have taken 250 pictures as he did his first time in Rocky Mountain National Park, but there were many worth 250 pictures. Standing atop the ridge over Goat Lake might be in their top three. Del Monte Ridge was there, too. Looking down the "glacier" at Home Lake, despite the fear in Colton's eyes, was a good one, as well. If even possible, a picture of "the fear in his eyes" could have won the prize. Other pictures looking up at various mountains would have been great as were the views. Colton's view from multiple angles while descending the mountain rapidly could be considered, but he didn't have a second opinion from said point of view – thankfully. His perspective had also been a bit rushed, as opposed to a traffic accident that seems to happen in slow motion.

As for wildlife, there were two kinds of creatures they actually saw – marmots (all over the place) and one black bear. Yes, they HEARD an elk and also a mountain goat. But they didn't count, as they were both unconfirmed. The bear, because of the rarity of seeing one, might win that category.

Note: Colton did find, once he was back in the world of the internet, more information. He learned that the marmots in the Olympics were their very own type – Olympic marmots. That may not have been enough to claim first place, but you couldn't find those critters anywhere else. And in another search on the 'net, Colton found that marmots had their own day in Alaska, beginning the year prior to their Olympic adventure. Marmot Day had replaced Groundhog Day. Different kind of marmot, though. There was no indication as to whether they favored more winter coming or the arrival of spring. And there was no movie about their day, so far as Colton could find. He also discovered that the Roosevelt Elk, the type found in the Olympic National Park area, are unique in that they live there and not many other places. They could be down into Oregon. Col had to check that out. He found out they were introduced to Kodiak, Alaska, and thereabouts, in the 1920's as well.

Best trail? Well … all of them? Even the non-trails? That was one huge tie. The hardest was probably the Goat Lake Way Trail. That was very difficult to maintain your footing on. The "non-trail" down to Royal Lake was a beast. And those were back-to-back.

Now for the "best moment" award … and there had to be multiple categories. Colton mentioned the second bottle of wine as a potential award winner. Bill noted this award was not for a "miracle", simply the best moment. To pick the very best, though, was one tough task. There could be at least one recognized every single day of the trip. Probably more than one. That category would have to be saved for another evening's discussion. The moon rise/sunset might be the winner.

The flight back was already ticketed. An "early" morning flight in Seattle (which is not THAT early, really) is a late morning or noonish flight when back on eastern time. Colton would burn the three hours he'd gained getting to Seattle. Essentially, half a day. Maybe less. Which was fine. He had nothing on his schedule at home, except for rest.

Chapter Twenty-Six

The Old Routine Tries to Kick In

⟶

Colton's great hiking and camping extravaganza was over. Life now would shift to normal.

His grand experiment to attempt camping before age 60 had been accomplished, with only months to spare. More than an attempt accomplished – a "goal" was met. Colton could scratch that off his bucket list, if, in fact, he had such a list, which he did not, and still doesn't. He looked at this feat and similar challenges as "goals" he desired, but not happenings that defined his life as successful (like a bucket list might for some people). Nevertheless, he had completed what he wanted to.

Now, he was on to his next accomplishment/goal – to kiss the most beautiful girl in the world, referencing a bucket list he had seen on some film (course, he needed to find her first). Might be that he had already found her, but maybe not. It was so, so subjective. It needed evaluation. Maybe he could help a complete stranger for the common good? Another bucket list item from the same movie. That would be something worth pursuing. Maybe he could make a charitable contribution to a worthy cause? And, one could argue that contributions made to certain organizations with a good purpose could help a stranger. Not sure the movie meant it in that way, but that was certainly possible.

Bill was kind enough to drop Colton at the airport. When they got to the car, Bill excused himself and ripped the plastic covering off Colton's seat.

"Forgot to do that yesterday," he said. "Sorry."

Colt was speechless (and that was rare), but he laughed. He hadn't even noticed it was on there when they arrived at the car from the trail.

Bill had Colton to the airport in time to check the bag of primarily toilet paper and a now well-used (or experienced) backpack and sleeping bag, along with a few items of clean clothes plus the tightly bound bag of clothes that just may end up being burned. Being a male, Colton had no extra shoes – no color options, no spares, nothing – just the hiking shoes that were now well-broken in. Not that he was criticizing ladies (or guys), who might take at least a second pair of shoes; they were just not an objective in his planning for most any trip (except in his "go to the gym" phase – which was short-lived and then long past its prime).

Bill took off for home, and Colton went on with airport check-in duties and all that. His bag was checked. And he hoped, again, that the baggage inspectors did NOT open that bag of horrifying clothes. He made his way through security, and there were no questions about the various scratches on his legs and arms. He was prepared with a tale of defending his life against a bear, but he wasn't required to practice that whopper of a story. And yes, he was somewhat disappointed.

Gate-waiting set in. There was no kissing anyone at the gate, and no charitable moment presented itself. The wait wasn't horribly long – just an hour or so. Too early to consume adult beverages, which wasn't a routine practice for Colton anyway. Now, it could be that he was cheap and adult beverages at the airport expensive. That could be …

Then, came a delay. About ninety minutes for some mechanical issue. Delays, while irritating, made sense, as a safe flight was his preferred flight. If they needed to replace an engine, go for it. He would wait. His connecting flight headed home was less of a concern, but it mattered, he supposed, and ninety minutes might kill that one and cause him to book a later flight. So, there could be a really-really long layover.

Delays for Colton were also opportunities to see what books were bestsellers, according to the bookstore at the airport, anyway. He had noticed that many times, they have them in order from number one to however many slots they have available, and there was always the possibility that he'd never heard of a few of them before. Occasionally, he had found an interesting one and bought it at an airport. Actually, he needed to spend more time looking for books than just when delayed by a flight, but he credited such a delay in finding "The Drunkard's

Walk: How Randomness Rules Our Lives" by Leonard Mlodinow. He had already read that one twice, after finding it the year before at an airport. He recommends that book. Said it's a good read. For this trip, there was one about a hornet's nest and a couple of political thrillers (or more) on the shelf. None really screamed, "BUY ME, COLTON!" And since his traveling days were now rare, he had found other outlets – better outlets – for finding new books, whether it be an e-book or a bound one.

And then, there was a second delay – another hour or so. The announcement mentioned trying to find another plane. That's never a good sign, is it? With that, Colton checked for options regarding other flights with connections to his home base. Must be a big eastbound day, as there were no empty seats on any flight. He couldn't even get within a few hours' drive of home so he could rent a car for the rest of the trip (and he had experience doing that before, but that one was a four-hour drive).

So …

Next, came the big announcement – his flight was canceled. Everyone was automatically booked for the next day on the same flight and same connections, unless your name was called (Colton's name was not called). Hopefully, the new flights scheduled didn't require a push-start and a pop of the clutch to get going.

But what about the rest of the current day?

Colton called Bill and asked about room availability, his nightly rate, transportation costs, and all information about expenses.

"No charge. That works for me to just come and get you, but I'm still fumigating the place where that bag of yours sat. I did finish the car. I can be there in an hour," Bill replied.

Did he really have to fumigate?

An hour worked for Colton, too. Airline employees were unloading bags from the crippled plane and sending them to baggage claim, as they would have to be rechecked the next day. A trip to baggage claim was then required. He hoped his bag wasn't covered with some thick, industrial plastic wrap with a warning label, similar to one you would see for radioactive stuff. It wasn't. And he didn't see any labels like, "Opened by TSA". In fact, his bag did not appear to have been opened, and it did not radiate any aroma one would want to mask up for. All was well. He also elected not to open the baggage and check on things – sometimes TSA puts a note inside a bag that they have opened it, versus a label on the outside that could fall off. The toilet paper bumps must not have been too suspicious.

And so, Colton waited for Bill to arrive.

Colton saw Bill's vehicle and started towards his car before he realized that Bill was wearing a gas mask. He must have been a Boy Scout in his earlier years and was prepared for such a moment. Colt didn't ask where he got the mask, but he did reassure him that his bag had apparently not been opened.

Well … it was back to Bill's.

"Went shopping – I have noodles for dinner," he said.

Colton had a look of faux anguish as Bill took the occasion to laugh. Maybe Bill was trying to even the score for all Col's gluten-free wisecracks. Or his singing. Rightfully so on either score.

Colton had at least one more change of clothes, could be for the evening (no black-tie event, he hoped), and then the same clothes for the flight the next day.

So, they discussed on the way, once again, to the bachelor pad, one more night of adventure and their options for one more meal. Elysian won the coin toss, if such a toss was even performed, mentally or otherwise.

Chapter Twenty-Seven

An Unexpected, Quickly Planned
Seattle Evening

There still had been no rain in Seattle. Must be a sign of the world ending … or something. *Could be a devilish hand involved, as opposed to the involvement you would expect from above?* Bill mentioned that they would avoid addresses for places that included 666, so as not to encourage any devilish notion. Seemed like a decent plan to Col. And the coin toss winner did not include that number, in whole or in part.

Colton recalled there was a newer red ale available at Elysian. The ale was named "Men's Room". The label did have a devilish look – which could substitute for the 666 number issue. There was a red devil with the appropriate tail, complete with an arrow at the end of said tail. They thought they might try a couple, or three – no more than four or five. Tops would be six. And food, but of course, no noodles. While not a huge burger eater, that sounded good to Colton. Bill could have one, too, and avoid gluten – no wheat bun, though, for him.

The next time they thought they might get together would be at a national underwriter meeting the following spring in Las Vegas. They had been to the one in the spring of 2010 in San Antonio, where the preparations for their huge hiking/camping extravaganza were pretty much finalized – at least as to the date such extravaganza would take place. If they could forecast enough plane malfunctions, they could head back to the trails that very week. But no, as they were out of noodles and had no plans to restock just yet.

As they sat there discussing the issues of gluten on the body, up walked a gentleman they sort of recognized, but he was out of place in their current setting. You know – you see a co-worker, from another area of the company, or someone with a business relationship, at the store and, in that environment, they just look "out of place". That was Col's thinking. Then, reality struck! It was one of the guys they had met along Royal Creek with his friends from Seattle and Idaho. There were re-introductions and a short chat. Col still could not recall his name. But, they found out that the brother and sister from Idaho had completed their mission with grandpa's ashes, and everyone had returned home. They only stayed one night out in the woods, due to heavy rain that came in about noon the next day. While sorry they'd had that experience, Bill and Colt thought they had lucked out – they were in Bill's car well before the rain arrived. And they'd never seen the weather coming.

The guy lived in Beacon Hill and was meeting the guy who lived closer to Bill, but Bill's nearly neighbor called to say he wasn't going to the pub as he was "under the weather". Must be raining where he lived. The Beacon Hill friend was then going to another place down the street to meet a lady. Colton and Bill pointed out that if he thought the lady would be more entertaining than them, well, okay, and they hoped he enjoyed his evening. He thought that might be the case and left them, despite never hearing Colton sing. Probably for the best.

Bill and Colton agreed that many people may come into your life and are then gone, some never to show up again. Sometimes, that was good – but you don't know until you know them or know them better. Sometimes, though, it might be too late, at least too late to make a smooth exit. If not for a plane issue, they may have never seen that guy again … well … Colton almost certainly would not have.

As for "out-of-place" people, Colton had a story ...

"I had gone to the grocery and had a cart, so the need must have been for more than, say, a loaf of bread."

"Or noodles," Bill offered.

"Yes – or noodles. Anyway, I turned down this aisle, and there was a representative from one of the service providers to my company. I forget where he lived then, but not in my area. He lived out of state somewhere. Took me a minute, and then the recognition kicked in, and I called him by name … which surprised me that I remembered. I asked what he was doing in my grocery as he had not called on the company in a while and wasn't scheduled to. Turns out, he had relatives east of town that he saw once a year or so, and the time had come for their gathering that year. But there was that delay in recognition that would not have come if we were at an industry meeting or the office."

"Every now and then I run into someone unexpected that I know, like at a concert or somewhere. Kind of catches you off guard a little," Bill noted.

Concerts. That reminded them of singing, for which Colton thought he may have had a bad rap, and that led to a discussion of musical events.

"Ever been to a house concert?" Bill asked.

"No. Never heard of such a thing. That excludes shower singing, I'm assuming?" Colton responded.

"Yes, shower singing is excluded. I have friends who get together at somebody's house to play. Kind of cool."

"The closest thing I have heard of that is a friend of mine from the early '90's who was dating a guy whose band rented a house just for practicing their music just a few blocks from where I lived at the time. I never went. Not so formal, like a 'concert' would be," Col said. "They must have been making enough money to justify the rental, so they must have been somewhat successful. Or had a write-off."

"There aren't any home events planned tonight that I know of for sure," Bill added. "Might have been an interesting experience to add to the adventures of the week."

"Maybe one of these days. Hard to fathom. Would be a more personal concert," Col responded, intrigued by the concept. "Is that more like a 'jam session,' so to speak?"

Bill suggested something somewhat different. "Sometimes, it's less formal, and a band or musician is interacting a lot with the attendees, more as one of them. Other times, they can be more formal, with introductions, breaks, food, drinks, and merch to buy, like CDs or shirts or whatever. No public service posters."

"Don't know if I could have ordered a public service poster that I would be personally proud of," Col offered.

The conversation turned to what was next coming up, if anything, besides work. Neither of them were entirely sure. Bill was going to do more climbing in the Cascades, which seemed more challenging than some of the Olympics – at least where he and his friends were going to climb. He was kind of anxious to see what was left of the snow in Deception Basin also, so a trip that way might be a reasonable consideration. Both ranges had spectacular scenery and great places to hunker down at night. Bill seemed satisfied with such excursions as being more of a hobby or weekend thing for him instead of his next job.

He mentioned a couple of the alternative places he had considered taking Colton. There was more to see and encounter in the Olympics. Much more. Colton thought he would like doing the camping thing again someday, like before he was 80. Or 75. Seventy might be too quick to plan for. That was only ten years away. He was not inclined to rush such a decision. He liked to plan just a few months before, and then hit the goal running, like trying to catch a flight. He was very comfortable with his health and so forth, and, if that continued, he wanted to find things to do that required slow, steady stamina, as opposed to major strength moves. Colton used biking as an example. He did not want to kill himself biking up a huge mountain or even a large hill, but he wouldn't mind going a hundred miles or more in a day, on a relatively flat terrain like some "rails-to-trails" paths. Most anyone could likely do that, but that was how Colton saw himself fitting into the biking world.

"Knowing your limits, even if self-imposed, I get that," Bill agreed. "You could always learn to swim. Or dance."

"Or sing," Colton said and smiled. "Just take the Flair pen with you."

"Do you ever remember getting a Flair pen with breakfast?"

"Honestly, I do not," Colton mused. "That cannot be retrieved from my memory banks. I used to use the pens … not all the time. I preferred fountain pens, back then. Did Flair pens come in more than black ink? Surely, they did."

"Don't remember. And it's 'Bill.'"

Colton sighed and said, "Yes … as soon as I said, 'surely'. I recalled 'Bill'. Loved that movie … 'Let's take some pictures…' And we took zero pictures on the excursion. Zero. Have to do this again – with pictures."

Bill was all for it. Before Colton was 70 would be great … or a little older than that … perhaps 75?

They then talked about music again – Col and Bill both loved music.

"And your favorite song – other than the Flair jingle?" Bill asked.

"Yes, of course … that one is not my number one. Picking number two is difficult because of all the various styles of music I like," Colton explained. "I guess number one for almost forty years, though, has been 'Imagine' by John Lennon. It's what is number two that gets really tough for me, I guess."

Colton rambled on about different performers he liked, some at certain times or when he was in certain moods. The closest he came to stating a number two was "Day is Done" by Peter, Paul and Mary. Bill, somehow able to stay awake during Colt's rambling, had what he called an eclectic taste in music – everything from the Dead to blues to jazz to classical. Colton admitted to having CDs from AC/DC to Dwight Yoakam (almost a to z) in his hundreds of CDs. They seemed to have another area of similarity, at least in the variety of music they appreciated, if not the same specific music.

And, so, the ninth day in the Seattle area, generally, was nearing an end. And there had been no noodles consumed for two days in a row. Life was good. There was no tent. No sleeping-bag. But there was a much better smelling presence.

It was back to Bill's for at least one more night, and then Colt would try to get back to some sense of reality. Or, perhaps a more apt description would be normalcy. Reality was present. It just wasn't his normal, everyday reality.

230

Chapter Twenty-Eight

The Old Routine Kicks In

The next morning, Bill dropped Colton at the airport to try once again to get the old man out of the state with that tightly wrapped bag of clothes before it cracked open. They didn't want that to happen, at least not in Bill's apartment.

Bag checked again, with the clothes tightly sealed, causing Colton a moment of thinking *Why didn't I just trash those clothes?* Heck, he might have to buy a new washer after running them through the one at home. He hoped not. He likely would never wear them again, anyway. Their usefulness had expired after an accomplished week. But no ... if satisfactorily cleaned, he could wear them as a conversation starter. "Do you know where I wore these clothes and what happened?" Another opportunity to discuss falling down a mountain, more likely introductions to and fighting off a bear, marmot watching, whatever. Noodles and oatmeal! And Col needed all the help he could get to start conversations. Once started, however, the listener/co-conversationalist was on their own to offer infamous words to Colt's ears, such as, "Oh, excuse me, I see a friend I haven't seen in minutes," or whatever other getaway comment was required to dislodge themselves from him.

Colton, despite public speaking now and then, was not a great conversationalist. There seemed to be wording under his name on any name tag he might be wearing that would say, "Just excuse yourself and move on – unless you can stand up while sleeping." Events without name tags had no warning. His personality was a rather shy one – at least when initially meeting new people. He sometimes tried to figure out how he was married three times. He didn't consider himself an outgoing person or an outstanding "catch", but he didn't mind being in front of a thousand people talking about life insurance underwriting issues or related topics. He honestly didn't think he captivated the ladies with risk-related banter, and that was likely true. "Let me tell you about my ten best risk assessments…" No, not a great way to draw them in.

Anyway, he was at the airport early. Still too early for sampling Elysian or anything close to that. The security checks were always shorter than predicted with rare exceptions, and that day was no different.

McDonald's was not offering Flair pens with breakfast. When he requested one, the order taker looked at Colton as if he had lost his mind. Were Flair pens even sold any longer? He did not know. Regardless, McDonald's wasn't giving them away that day. Seems like that they could have offered a "McFlair" as a promotional item. They could have moved on to gel pens from felt-tipped ones, he supposed. Colton wondered if there was a jingle for whatever gel pen they may have adopted. If there was, he had missed it. Colton, himself, had pretty much moved on from memorizing advertising jingles.

He had time to check for books again. But guess what? There was no change from the day prior – none that was obvious to him. You would think one book would have moved ahead of another or something although, no, he did not remember the exact order. Perhaps it was a weekly change – made more sense. Or even a monthly reset. Not having memorized them or written them down, he could not really verify that the order was the same.

He made his way to the gate. And there was no delay. They must have changed the engine … or the plane. *Hope they got all the bolts on tight,* he thought.

He figured it would be a good flight on which to close his eyes, although he never experienced good sleep on any flight that he could recall. Ever. He was never inclined to chat with fellow passengers much. The shyness thing could have been a big factor, or the inability to come up with more than, "Hi". He always did better if he was in a group of his underwriting people or with another of his personal interest groups, which was rare, or he knew the person seated beside him.

Once, he recognized the guy across the aisle from him on one of those smaller planes. He couldn't remember the year, but thought the flight had to be when the gentleman was still the hockey coach at a Big Ten school.

He said to the coach, "You look like someone who knows a lot about hockey."

"Well, there are many people who would disagree with you!" the coach replied.

They then talked the entire flight about Big Ten sports, including Indiana University basketball.

Colton also recalled once chatting with a flight attendant. He had been reading a book by Stephen Hawking. He couldn't remember which one. Anyway, the attendant came up to him as he was closing the book and putting his head back to stop the spinning.

"Good book … I enjoyed it," she said, "but I had to take a break now and then, too."

They definitely agreed on the complexity of the book.

The plane from Seattle took off on time. There was no unusual vibration. All was good.

Colton was headed back for a late afternoon arrival, after one short layover. The connection was decent so long as the first flight took off on time – and it did. He had no real concern about the second flight taking off early.

While thinking back over the week's events – well, really, the past nine days of happenings – Colt realized that this was the first national park he had been to where he had not gone to some sort of visitor's center, gift shop, or other official building. There was the "welcome" sign in the middle of the woods on the one trail that signaled he and Bill were entering Olympic National Park. But no drop box for an entry fee was found. There was included on the sign the new rules once you took the next step, but that was mostly about campfires, if he remembered correctly. If need be, a visit to some sort of official building could be on his list of reasons to go back some day.

He needed pictures, too. At least 250 …

Well, no, not 250 pictures. Colton claimed that over the years, using his phone as a camera had helped him refine pictures by deleting them, re-taking them as needed, or just the reconsideration of what pictures to take to begin with. The Fugi camera he still owned, but had not used much for years, could be used the same way, but it was something else to carry. It seemed like camping and hiking called for the phone as a camera, at least for him. The Fugi wasn't huge, but it was larger than his phone and a little heavier. He also thought his phone might take better pictures and had more zoom capability over the Fugi.

The plane landed successfully. And then, he had a short wait for his connecting flight. The bookstore there had the same books as Seattle, as far as he could tell. Not that he had made a list or committed one to memory, even the second day he was there in Seattle, but they seemed to be the same. Nothing jumped out at him. He guessed the rankings weren't regionalized or else we were all just reading the same books across the country. Good to know, perhaps. So, airports could determine bestseller lists, and that claim by a newspaper on the east coast was a fraud? Weird thoughts for a harried traveler.

His connection was made. He didn't miss the flight because he was reviewing books available.

Colton could not remember the arrival at his home base airport. He had done that so many times, they all ran together. It was pretty uneventful, for the most part. It was a small airport. The gift shop wasn't even open every day.

He arrived home. His dogs were thrilled. They were happy after a 20-minute separation, so this was a biggie. Indy was barking like crazy, must have been trying to tell Dad something. Myna was making more of a crying noise – a very happy cry, more a higher pitched bark or something like that. And Myna always greeted Dad the same way. When she was a puppy, she would run around one of his legs, either one. As a grown dog, now somewhat taller, she still liked to "run" between his legs to greet him. She had decided that was the way you greet every human … with just a poke here and there.

His bag of clothes would remain unopened until the house was completely void of people. It was probably best to open it outside, where there were no neighbors downwind. "Garbage bag" would be the correct label.

Life was good. Well, there was his thumb …

Chapter Twenty-Nine

An Epilogue?

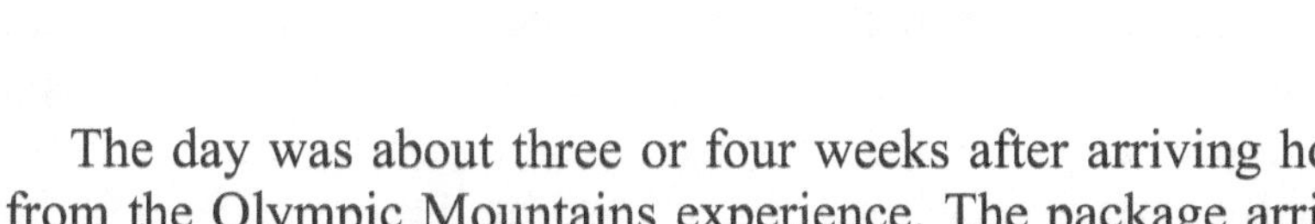

The day was about three or four weeks after arriving home from the Olympic Mountains experience. The package arrived addressed to Colton with his name grossly misspelled as something like "Clinton" and a mangled last name. There was no return address. Inside was a bag of noodles … so it was not too hard to name a suspect. There was no gift card enclosed.

For roughly seven years, the bag of noodles would unceremoniously show up at Bill's or Colton's. Back and forth. Not right away, of course. Well, once in a while. With a coming holiday, maybe the anniversary of their hike in the woods, possibly a birthday. Not on any particular schedule. And not usually repeated in said timing as to avoid any semblance of order or predictability. Just whenever. Colton eventually had to take the blame for the end of the anonymous gifting, as he lost the noodles in a move when his third spouse couldn't let go of what was called "the boating incident" and left Colton to take care of the dogs by himself. Sad, perhaps – the loss of the bag of noodles. That could have possibly saved the postal service from any financial issue it had over the years that followed.

If dehydrated marmot ever becomes a thing, then a new mailing happens. Colton thought that didn't have to be an Olympic marmot – most any marmot would do just fine. An Olympic marmot, however, would be absolutely perfect! *Let's not start one with oatmeal,* he thought. He likely would prefer to eat that versus ship it back.

Looking back occasionally, the event in the woods and mountains was quite the experience. And it remained so – one of his best. Colton's, that is. Bill couldn't get the jingle out of his head, and his rumored therapy seemed to be going well because of that. Bill still loved the campsite on top of the ridge the second night of the seven, and that helped somewhat set aside the terror of Colton's voice trashing the jingle. At least he was finally able to return to work, but he took a different route, so he would not pass a certain fast-food restaurant. *Probably best.*

Dehydrated marmot …

For Colton, he finally ate noodles again. That was a few years out. He could not understand why he never felt bloated by the "trail noodles", but usually felt sufficiently stuffed with other kinds. Noodles, which he thought he liked that first night in the woods, finally made a return.

Could be gluten … or gluten free … he didn't care which.

Anyway, yes, there were a few years and then spaghetti and other noodle-like dishes started to ease their way back into the Col Diet. He didn't need therapy. His resistance to eating them for a while helped him, whereas a jingle that would break into your consciousness, not set to a pattern of occurrence like a meal, but rather could just happen out of the blue, was more difficult to manage in everyday life without therapy … apparently … ask Bill.

They still speak and write each other, despite the need for therapy (claimed by Bill). Colt just knows that he never starts a paragraph or sentence, when speaking with or writing Bill, with the word "breakfast". Period. Never. Having control of that means that Colton can no longer test the therapeutic status with a single word especially when speaking and saying the word as "brrreakfast…" That would just be cruel.

The question of his height was gradually set aside. The blame for his stature could not be attributed to anyone. Colton actually became fascinated at times by the question of his ancestry and built a very nice family tree on his mom's side. He had little information on his dad, other than a name, and was unable to build that tree beyond grandparents and a few relatives. Very disappointing.

Primarily using Ancestry.com for the tree led to a passing interest in DNA testing, as that became available, knowing that the test results would not necessarily help build the tree, although they might validate a direction for his search. Well, he did it, but the results were perplexing. They did not validate anything he had been told about his dad's family, nor really his mom's family, to some extent. There was very little Germanic influence found, for example. And to further confuse him, there were DNA "matches" for first and second cousins from a totally different family. The murkiness back there, from years later, was becoming more apparent. Turns out the "new family", with the cousins and matching DNA, did not have six footers. So, was the mystery then solved regarding his height? Or was it not? Uncertainty still reigns.

As for his music, Colton added more CDs over the years, and he finally added a "Z" artist – Natalia Zukerman. Now he has "A to Z" in his CD collection. He told me that the lady also does art, like pet portraits and murals. Col never had her paint a picture or pictures of his dogs. How did he know of and then meet her? At a home concert – he finally attended some and then had his own as well!

Colton still has and wears his hiking boots, especially in winter when hiking in the woods where he now lives. They might help deflect low biting snakes or ankle-biting dogs. The 43P 14844 187XXX boots had consecutive numbers, left and right (kind of like credit card numbers – hiding part of the number with X's). The numbers are on the tongues of the boot – he thought "43" was the size (a big number), "P" he wasn't sure about (and did not research, at all), and the rest may have been a serial number. He never investigated it as a whole. But, as of this writing, he's still wearing them. The only issue? The pull loop on the back of the left boot. The loop broke. Colton had that fixed once. And then the thing broke again, and now it just flops around on the back of the boot, sometimes tucked in for whatever reason. That works. But either way, he never used them as pulls that he remembered, but maybe he did, and that's why the loop eventually broke. So, he quit doing that. Took five years or so to fail, though. *Good boots.*

And size 43 – that number pumped up the short, non-athlete for just a fraction of a second, while thinking that a lot of NBA players have lower numbers as a shoe size. Now then, that wouldn't be a great conversation starter, would it? Wouldn't for sure mean much in Europe, right?

Colt has a scar on his left thigh – he says – in honor of his slide down the hill. He doesn't show that off very often, if at all. He may have never shown it off. He offered to show me "for the record", but I said, "No, no … that's okay … I believe you, and I likely have one very eerily similar." No comparison was ever made. Col doesn't talk about the "snow fall" very much anymore, or the scar. Other temporary scars (or cuts that fully healed – so non-scars) were on his lower left and right legs. He couldn't recall if there were any on his arms, but, if there were, they were all well healed. There was no impaling to acknowledge. That would have been tough to exaggerate, although Col used to work with a guy who would have tried or just lied about the wound – like how close one came to the liver and the other to the pancreas … that sort of thing.

Colt insists the hiking and camping extravaganza in the Olympic Mountains of Washington was one of the best experiences of his life and remains so, over ten years later. That was the only life story he attempted telling a storyteller in detail (so far) in order that this story could possibly be printed. The storyteller – that's me – told him that his shortness alone would not be a good book length topic (it was, wait for it, too short) and neither would his non-athleticism or snake history. No. None of that. He thought that driving the Indy car could be, if adequately embellished. And I sort of weakly agreed, but initially said that would not fit anywhere in this treatise. (So, to his credit, he figured out a way to include that…) Maybe that's another short story, but not a book. An essay? Perhaps. Now, the dogs could be an entire book and could be an embellished part truth, part fiction effort. That might be next time, after the Indy car one … or before. Not at all is also a big possibility. Col tells me that the dogs are both gone now, and they're missed a lot.

Yes, some parts of this story are purportedly true, some parts are likely exaggerations, some are purely fiction. Not sure which is which, as Colton rambles pretty well, and he did so constantly in describing the tale, with changes now and then as well. Or did he call them "corrections"? Maybe "clarifications". Still, a weave of a story that was fun to witness the telling of while making notes to try to create a short book. As mused about above, it makes me want to explore more of what might be in Colton's memory that could be told and then adjusted or fictionalized as needed to make the story (or stories) semi-presentable – old people have a lot of experiences sometimes not properly explored. The reason he was able to do so much with his mom's ancestry was because he sat down and talked with his grandma, taking notes on names and relationships. Turns out, everything she provided Colton was confirmed eventually through record searches on Ancestry.

And remember, Col is a little shy, too. His shyness reminded me of the girl who supposedly warned him of that first snake at that state park years ago. Was that really a "warning" or merely an attempt to assist the shy teenager by offering a "conversation starter"? Or was the warning an effort to establish a debt owed to the young lady for "saving his life"? Perchance she was, indeed, interested in the young man, but needed an assist to gain his interest, since he was not going to explore any interest on his own. The innocent teen, Col, might have had no idea what to say. Well, apparently the effort, if so intended to create some opening for the girl, did not work. Either it went over his head, or he fumbled the opportunity by making some lame comments, exaggerated ones at that. And he may have had on that special name tag, and she could not sleep standing up. This will never be known. *How did he ever end up married? And three times? Even once? Golly.*

Speaking of marriage, Colton told me that Bill ended up marrying – get ready for this one – an IU girl. Indiana University. Ain't life grand? A prediction that actually came about!

Several weeks after the seven-day event in the woods with Colt, Bill and some of his climbing friends went back through the Home Lake area, Constance Pass, and Del Monte Ridge, where Colton had taken the mountainside tumble. The "area of loose footing", you remember? Had to check Deception Basin, he guessed. They found the tree where Colt landed on that fall down the mountain. A fitting gift was there from some bear in the form of bear scat. Berries. No bells or smell of pepper.

Life was (and is) good … well … except for his thumb …

Everett Kunzelman

244

Note From Everett "Ev" Kunzelman

Thank you for reading my first effort at a novel, a historic one at that.

Within this novel are true events described, some exaggerated ones even further embellished and then there is some (or much) pure fiction. "Colton" (or "Colt" or "Col") is a fictious character that has a lot of life parallels with someone I know fairly well and the story is "as told by" the fictional character to me, the storyteller. This was a great project intertwining the reality of a similar hiking and camping experience I had with the fantasy of an adventure that could have been very likely to have occurred.

I am hopeful this short novel made you think about events of your life and what was or possibly was or could have been with a change here and there. Dreaming and imagining are not terrible activities. I've read that memories sometime "evolve" as we experience something new and that may not be awful either.

Feedback is welcome. You can send me comments via Messenger at m.me/everettkunzelman or through email at ewk1642@outlook.com. And please visit my website at www.oneretiredguy.com.

Again, thank you so much for reading! – *Ev*

Everett Kunzelman

Acknowledgements

Thanks to my real partner in my hiking and camping extravaganza, Bill Fleming, for helping me survive my personal experience and for assisting in the descriptions of the trails he knows so well in the Olympic Mountains as well as reading the novel and providing input. Thanks to my other "readers," Bob Todd and Leah Craig, for spending their valuable time taking a good look at the story and providing assistance. Thanks to my editor, D. D. Scott, who also had to read the novel and provide help in capturing the moments for readers to enjoy, but also pushed the writer to take one of his short, true stories and expand that.

About the Author

After a brief editing "career" of a few months at a magazine experiencing financial woes, the relatively new college graduate sought out a temporary job to hold him over until his writing career could be reestablished. About 45 years later, after rewarding experiences within the life insurance risk selection profession, the writing effort recommenced with his first attempt at a book in 2019. There are articles out there by the author on diabetes, renal failure and other matters dealing with risk selection, but those were a part of his professional participation that included his selection to the Association of Home Office Underwriter's "Hall of Fame" in 2020. The career was exciting, but there is so much more to share.

Beyond the life insurance industry, there were the years adding to a life well-lived, creating so much material for essays and the basis for storytelling beyond "work." This time is dedicated to his dogs (all Goldendoodles, including Dawson – she was adopted in September 2021 – and his two, Izzy and Maya, who are no longer with us), his family, his many friends, and his hope for a better world and a better life.

Everett Kunzelman

Books by the Author

[Three previous plus this one ... as noted below ...]

One Retired Guy
(Humorous Essays on Life After Retirement):

One Retired Guy & His BFFs: His Dogs, His Garage and
His Cabin in the Woods
(Humorous Essays on Life After Retirement - Collection 1)

One Retired Guy's Guide to the Holidays
(Humorous Essays on Holiday Life After Retirement)

One Retired Guy: Life Re-examined
(Humorous Essays on Life After Retirement – Collection 2)

More Coming Soon!